Gwd.

J (L) (3-08) ✓

(R2C)

S0-AYT-285

HODDER GOES HOME

Mitch Hodder returns to his home town after twenty years in prison for gunning down the man who murdered his father. A member of a gang of bank robbers, his father had been entrusted with burying the proceeds of a robbery and had died trying to stop one member of the gang double-crossing the rest. Only Hodder now knows where the gold is, but brutal Clem Mathers and his gang are waiting for him when he gets out . . .

VANCE MACKENZIE

HODDER GOES HOME

Complete and Unabridged

LINFORD
Leicester

First published in Great Britain in 1992 by
Robert Hale Limited
London

First Linford Edition
published 1997
by arrangement with
Robert Hale Limited
London

British Library CIP Data

Mackenzie, Vance
Hodder goes home.—Large print ed.—
Linford western library
1. Western stories
2. Large type books
I. Title
823.9'14 [F]

ISBN 0–7089–5091–4

Published by
F. A. Thorpe (Publishing) Ltd.
Anstey, Leicestershire

Set by Words & Graphics Ltd.
Anstey, Leicestershire
Printed and bound in Great Britain by
T. J. International Ltd., Padstow, Cornwall

This book is printed on acid-free paper

1

HIS black dust-filled eyes narrowed as he caught a distant gleam across the vast, purpling plain. Almost unwillingly he grimaced; a mirthless smile that acknowledged the fear and excitement mounting inside him, as it did every time he got some proof he was being followed.

Someone was out there. Someone as patient as himself. Someone as alert and remorseless. He knew who.

He remained tautly immobile as the sun sank lower, staring at the landscape giving way to impenetrable shadows. The day had been hot; now the breeze which was getting up was dry and cooling. But there was nothing in this hard vastness to yield to the wind. Only far-off specks of circling buzzards moved.

His eyes stayed on the horizon,

straining, as were all his senses, to pick up further signs. How many of them were there? he most wanted to know. He'd heard talk last night in Hargreaves of two strangers arriving late but he guessed there'd be more.

A night's hard riding now would put some further distance between himself and his trackers. He could move faster than them in the dark. And by dawn his trail would be cooling. Steadfastly he hauled himself back into the saddle, wincing as a needle of pain lanced through his right shoulder.

An old wound may heal but it will never disappear completely.

He would lose them for the moment, but then they knew where he was ultimately heading. This time tomorrow they'd be out there at his back as usual. Tomorrow he would not be moving on, however.

Dawn was breaking as the mounted figure approached the outskirts of the busy township of Ashton, passing the first of the railroad company's corral-yards and cattle-pens. Somewhere beyond a rooster crowed.

At length he entered the wide main street and let the grey-brown stallion pick its way wearily through the thick dust and wheel ruts. Had any eyes been watching they would have seen the approach of a brown rider, tall in the saddle but trim and at one with the horse which was as thick with dust as himself.

His face was shaded by the low-crowned, wide-brimmed stetson, brown in colour. His clothes, too, on his tall and wiry frame, were of the same featureless dun: a brown leather jacket, creased and sweat-stained, a tawny shirt and buff denim pants worn over tan riding boots conspicuous only for their length of spur.

Around his middle a broad, cartridge-clustered leather belt slanted, bearing a holster with the plain ivory grips of a revolver sticking out. He was a man of very few words. A man of business. Everything proclaimed him as such.

There was nothing on him, nothing about him, which was in any way fancy or superfluous. And, naturally, the right side of his unbuttoned jacket was pulled back for access to the heavy Colt.

The single trace of brightness was a yellow neckerchief loosely worn at his throat.

Only when he dismounted and straightened up stiffly was it apparent that he, like his dress, was brownish — a russet Indian colour. Yet he had the features of a white man; they were lean, keen and alive and his black eyes were like living coals of fire. They burned out of his head as though in defiance of the world. It was a proud and handsome face all right, but it had known infinite troubles.

★ ★ ★

A man was perched on a chair behind the counter so that all that was visible of him were the narrow shoulders and a grey face skull-capped with whitish

4

hair plastered down with perspiration.

He looked the type to enjoy turning his ferrety little eyes on anyone that he felt was beneath him. He cleared his throat but it was only preparatory to an immense expectoration which clanged into an unseen spittoon.

He resumed his reading, as though Mitch was invisible.

The visitor had become used to this kind of welcome. If a white man was to walk in now, especially a well-heeled one, the counter-jumper's expression might change. He might part his thin, bloodless lips a little and force the semblance of a crooked smile.

Mitch understood the rules. He began his usual speech, well-honed in dozens of similar joints over the last few months. He needed a room, a tub, some food, a livery-stable. He was riding through and might be a night or two. He took out his roll and offered to pay in advance. This usually did the trick.

There was a weird upturn of the

other man's lips now but only his mouth was smiling — half smiling.

He took the money, folded it and breast-pocketed it. Suddenly, as though on a whim, he took something out of a drawer.

"You been on the trail long, boy?" He was now toying with a brass key in his boney hands as though reluctant to hand it over.

"Yep!"

"Travellin' by yerself?"

Mitch put his hand out for the key. If anything, the wizened man seemed to have taken it further away.

With one decisive move Mitch had grabbed the man's hand and started to pressure it. The key fell to the counter.

"That ain't funny, mister." The man's face was now still with hate. His eyes seemed to have darkened, with pain perhaps. "That ain't funny one bit."

"Friend, I've never been known for a sense of humour. Or for wasting time with cheapskates . . . "

The quiet menace in Mitch's voice had frightened the man, who was moistening his lips and shifting around uncomfortably. A corner of his mouth had started to quiver.

"Room Seven, two flights up," he was saying, "and the livery's across the street."

Mitch nodded almost sympathetically at the man still wringing his hands.

"Thanks friend," he said, with no bitterness in his voice.

★ ★ ★

Once in his hotel room he made no attempt to sleep because he had somewhere to go.

He took everything in at a glance. A heavy table occupied most of the space by the window. This pleased him in that it could be tilted to provide cover in the event of a shoot-out. There were small, scattered luxuries which he had no time for — cushions on the chair, flowered curtains at the window, a red carpet. He was staying at the best hotel in town.

He put his gunbelt down on the bed whilst he poured water from a large jug into the bowl and started to wash off.

Very soon he had shaved and breakfasted and was out on the street, walking determinedly.

He barely knew his way because the town had grown so fast in the years he'd been away. When he'd been a boy there'd not been much more than one main street, dirty during summer and awash with mud when the rains came. Now there were clusters of streets and everywhere warehouses crowded next to stockyards. The sleepy town had been transformed — to him it seemed — overnight.

Apart from the clang-clang-clang from the smithy there had formerly been little noise of industry. Now every so often above a thousand clashing sounds he could hear the whistle of an engine from the freighthead.

8

Like so many Western towns Ashton had begun as a mere trading post, quickly becoming heavily fortified — a paranoiad little place — and then gradually growing in size as people flocked to it for protection.

There were Apaches to the north, brooding and smouldering atop their huge canyon fastnesses, natural fortresses with insurmountable craggy battlements. Occasionally, when the mood or the moon took them, these Apaches would come skirmishing down, as would the Commanches from their eastern escarpments. There were rustlers, too, bands of ruthless, ugly men who sometimes came to carry off more than cattle.

But this had all been in the early days before the war. After that fateful period the town had consolidated and then begun to grow in every direction, becoming even more prosperous as a frontier post.

Hardly a day went by without soldiers, homesteaders and travelling men coming through, sometimes in their hundreds, in great wagon trains whose dust signalled their arrival an hour in advance.

Many stayed on. They liked what they saw after the miles of scrub, rock and more barren rock and scrub. Jack Hodder, an Englishman from Bristol, had been one of them, bringing with him the Indian bride he had picked up on the trail, traded for an ancient Remington and a bottle of malt.

It was a pleasant place all right, this oasis in a stony desert. It was on account of the spring; Manywells Spring they called it, and it never failed. Round the town was good, verdant cattle land, the best you'd find for a week's ride in any direction, it was said.

There was no shortage of jobs for cattlemen and cowboys as the ranches grew in size. And wherever you find men like that women are not far behind. So the good people of Ashton bred and so did the bad and by the time Mitch

Hodder was returning it was a thriving community, one of the largest in the territory.

He made his way up the hill and eventually found what he was looking for. Below the wooden cross in the middle of the graveyard there was a half-obliterated inscription. The name Jack Hodder was still decipherable — just. But there was no cross for his mother who, he had been informed in prison, had died seventeen years ago. As an Indian she would not have been buried here near to the Bethel. Mitch thoughtfully picked up and held to his nose a yellow flower, one of a bunch which had recently been placed at the head of the grave.

He spun round and walked doggedly down the track, the town below him. No, it had not changed, he thought. For all its differences it was the same town he had been brought up in. As he came back to the centre he saw the same school-house where he'd received the little book-learning he had. The

Cotton Tree, it had always been called because of the white fluffy flowers it bore in summer, was still standing at the corner of Main Street, falling forward even more than it had used to. It was here that the youth of Ashton would hang around and taunt him as he passed about his parentage and his skin. Yes, this was the same town that had betrayed him and sent him at gunpoint to a prison a thousand miles away.

He lay on the lumpy bed but could not sleep. His mind and body ached with weariness but he wondered if he would ever sleep properly again till this was all over.

Why the men had followed him he could not exactly figure. Would all of them be out there now? Could they all have survived twenty long years? Longer for him looking up at the iron bars each day — but safer. He could not imagine that those four, Crag Stevens, Hemp Martindale, Clem Mathers and the worst, the psychopathic killer Clay

Beaver, could all have gone through life unscathed. Not if they were as his pa had described them.

There would have been other banks to rob, other shootings, and inevitable casualties. Unless — unless, of course, they'd all turned their backs on crime. Maybe they had. Perhaps they'd all felt so mighty relieved to have gotten away with the biggest bank raid in the territory, to say nothing of three killings. Maybe they'd decided to stick it out, wait for the kid to get out of jail, knowing he'd go back for the money which wasn't his but which his father had paid for with his life and which he, himself, had earned with the sweat of penal servitude.

So they'd followed him. All the way from Arizona. Sticking close to him but determined not to be seen.

They must have known the date of his release. Of course they'd have taken the trouble to find out. They might have had to bribe some prison official to get to know, but with big bucks at stake there would be no difficulty getting such apparently inconsequential information.

Then they'd pursued him overland, always half a ride behind him. They must be good, very good. But then they'd known his direction and that by whatever rambling and shambling route he chose and however long he stopped on the way to earn a grubstake, he was heading north back to Ashton.

He marvelled at their patience. Only back home would he have the single advantage over them. He knew where the gold was; he and he alone had seen his pa bury it. They couldn't be sure of anything, except that it was hidden somewhere between Hargreaves, above which town the gang had been holed up, and Ashton, where his pa had lived. That was their only certain knowledge apart from the fact that at some stage Jack must have told his 17-year-old son where he'd cached it.

They could not know that Mitch had been present at the hiding of the money. Had they known that they wouldn't have trailed him all the way to Hargreaves. They'd have been sitting pretty in Ashton, waiting for him to arrive.

No one knew he'd helped to bury the money, except perhaps Jenny who might have guessed it. And if she'd guessed it, might she not have figured where he'd led his pa to hide it . . . ? This was a thought that had tormented him many times.

2

THE wind of the descent caught her long golden hair and it streamed out, softly brushing against his face. She sat close to him, bumping against him, clinging to him, occasionally screaming — in pleasure not terror.

At the bottom of the steep gulley he reined back the old draught horse and the creaking, rocking buckboard came to a halt.

She clambered into the back obligingly as she always did and lay down on the warped and cracked, grain-prickly boards, her eyes wide and shining. He threw after her the old rug, a patchwork of cut strips, which she'd been sitting on.

She held her breath while he undid the lacing at her cleavage. He did this automatically while gazing down

16

into her eyes. The late-afternoon sun's rays, spearing through the scrubby trees' cover, blazed on her hair. Her lips were parted in a soft smile; her beauty seemed the greater for her sandy freckles.

"Ain't it hard," she drawled.

"What?" he asked absently. It was a joke she always used.

"Workin' for ol' man Martin." She giggled slightly. "He never gives you a minute."

They both laughed.

"Aye," he said, cupping her firm young breasts in his hands, "at the moment he thinks I'm out deliverin' down at the Leggat spread."

Then he bit her neck with his lips, not his teeth, and they'd done talking.

★ ★ ★

With a twitch he awoke. Immediately he was bolt upright and striding to the window. He looked up at the wide sky which was navy-blue and dusted with

17

stars. He'd been asleep all day.

Down below two men were just arriving. They were older than himself, one heavy and belly-plump, the other lean and ascetic. Mitch rested his chin on the palms of his hands and watched them dismount. Their horses were well-travelled. He felt a sudden gripe in the pit of his stomach.

These might be two of the original gang. Which two? he wondered. Or they might be two horsemen riding through.

Then the big one looked up, and Mitch recognized him. He'd seen him in a courthouse a long time ago. He'd been slimmer then.

The man was mean-looking with a flattened nose. Mitch comforted himself with the thought that the heavy-jowled, round face, thick lips parted and bushy eyebrows raised, was that of a stupid man.

It was the second traveller who sent another visceral surge through him just as he had at the trial twenty years back. His was a thin face and his eyes, protuberant as though from constant vigilance, were taking the whole street in, and every window.

"Clem Mathers," breathed Mitch as he drew back into the shadows of his room.

He did not know how he knew it, but somehow he was certain. This was Mathers; it had to be. Not that his pa had ever described him physically, but he had always mentioned his name with awe mingled with fear. There was something in that face down there which gave a similar sensation to Mitch. It was the face of a man who never did anything without a purpose and a plan.

Mitch waited for them to disappear then leaned out of the window to get a better look at their horses, a black and a grey. He would know them if he saw them again. Such knowledge might prove decisive. And he had the feeling that his horse, when rested, could outride the two of them.

He went out.

★ ★ ★

He saw the shack in the darkness. While so many fine new buildings had gone up in the town it was perhaps no surprise that this, out at the point, seemed to have been so badly neglected and abandoned. It was smaller than he remembered it. Its fence had fallen down and it looked as though there must have been some subsidence. It had been empty for years.

His mind went back to that morning so many mornings ago when he'd been sitting on the porch swing and seen his pa in the distance riding one horse with, strangely, another in tow.

His pa had been smiling with pleasure at seeing his pretty, red-brown squaw and his growing boy, after two months away. He was smiling all right, but when that wore off there was fear and neglect etched into his countenance.

The gang had let him go with the money not because he was the leader — that was Clem Mathers — but because he was the only one who could be trusted. By nature he was a trustworthy man as far as bank robbers go but the difference between himself and the others was that he was married and had a child. He would not betray them because his family were dead if he did. He'd driven overnight through the cross canyon, moving slowly because of the weight of gold his horse was carrying and because he had another horse in tow, also carrying gold.

It had been a perfect robbery, his pa told him as they drove off to stash the loot. It had been perfect by design because Clem Mathers was a clever man, but also perfect in the way it had turned out, with luck being on their side and all.

They'd robbed the bank at Bucksville, a bank which, it had been said, could not be robbed. Many had tried, but had bitten the dust on the street outside, or had been gunned down remorselessly either by the pursuing posse or by those waiting along the trail, alerted by the telegraph and knowing that the bank robbers would be going south to Mexico hoping to out-distance their followers.

But Clem's plan had been brilliant: head south and then wheel round, actually in a horse-shoe movement, eventually heading due north to the hills, where, even if they were followed, they could hide up till the heat was off.

But that was only the getaway. Weeks of planning had gone into it. All six members of the gang had arrived well in advance and at different times, the first a full fortnight before Hemp Martindale, the last to arrive. They came as drifting cowboys and got jobs. But on the 1st of October they were to meet up again to rob the bank. It needed six guns to do it, five inside and one man out holding the horses. There was so much gold in those vaults nothing less than six horses could carry it. The bad luck was that they had to kill a bank teller and two men.

Beaver had gunned all three down,

saying that they'd gone for their guns. Afterwards no one had argued with him, but Mitch recalled his father saying he thought that at least one of the dead men wasn't even packing.

But then they had good luck on their side. Normally it would take the sheriff a good twenty minutes to raise a posse and be on the trail. Men couldn't just leap on horseback. They had to saddle up and check their equipment. They had to take enough provisions with them for several days riding because there was no point setting off after raiders unless you were determined to keep going as long as they could. But, on this particular morning, Sheriff Danver and his men were unusually difficult to raise — and so were their horses because they had been out all night after rumours of Indians lurking in the hills. So the posse, starting out late, were unable to keep up the furious pace of the robbers who had a further ace in the hole. They had fresh mounts which

Martindale had hobbled only two days before. Thus in good spirits and on sleek horses the outlaws had begun the sweep north which had completely baffled the sheriff.

* * *

Her perfume was musky and seductive in the flickering half-light. Her hair was raven and she had beautiful dark brown eyes with long black lashes. Her skin was pale; her lips were lusciously painted the colour of the red satin dress she was wearing.

Before words had been exchanged she had put her hands on his shoulders, drawing him to her. She was beautiful but she was insolent. She had the pert insolence of a woman who night after night welcomes different men to her bed and knows there'll be more tomorrow. She knew her power.

He was trembling urgent; he did not take long.

Afterwards she said, "You'll be leaving

tomorrow, I guess?"

He smiled faintly. "No, I'm gonna stick around."

She looked at him with perhaps a little more interest.

"You're new to these parts?"

"I've passed this way before," he said, meaning to give little away. She looked and smiled, prompting him to say more. "A good few years ago now," he added.

"Ah," she said.

She was at the mirror now, putting on more lip-paint by the light of two candles at either end of the dressing table, but she was watching him all the while.

"Have you any reason for staying?" she asked. "Business, maybe?"

"Yeh, business," he said vacantly.

He was drawing on his boots.

"Then you'll be stayin' till Mr Bellow can see you, then? All business goes through him in these parts."

Bellow: the name was strangely familiar. Yes; he remembered that

Slim Bellow had kept the grain store, but he'd be pushing eighty now and he'd hardly been the ambitious type.

But then old Slim had had a son. Mitch searched hard to remember the name of the tousle-haired lad who'd been two or three years younger than himself.

"Would that be Jed Bellow?" he enquired. "Would that be Jed Bellow?" she mimicked. "As if he didn't know."

She seemed for a moment to be talking to some third person.

Mitch smiled again.

She lit herself a half-smoked black cheroot, which had been lying in an ash-tray, and dragged the smoke a long way down before fixing him with a stare.

"Have you come here to kill him?"

He stood up sharply. "No, no," he found himself saying. It was absurd to be denying such a stupid accusation but the last thing he wanted was to get involved unnecessarily, or to be thought involved. "Why do you say that?"

"You look the type to take on the odds."

He gave a bitter laugh.

She gently pushed him to sit down on the bed again and was beside him, her long fingers picking nervously at the blanket.

"I wouldn't tell if you were," she said.

For a second he glimpsed the little girl she had once been. Her professional hardness had momentarily dissipated. There would be softenings like this when her heart, which had been hardened by life, by her calling, by the unshorn, unwashed men who passed through her hands, would melt. For a time she'd be kind and generous — but never trusting.

He got to his feet again and reached for his hat.

"There ain't no hurry," she said. "I kinda like you. You can stay some. Most men take a lot longer."

"I'll call again — maybe."

Her mouth hardened.

"All right, cowboy," she said, cool and impersonal once more. "You do that. Don't you forget to ask for Maisie, now."

"Maisie," he repeated.

Quickly he went down the stairs and tipped the old hag who opened and closed the door for clients. He found himself face to face on the boardwalk with one of the men he'd seen earlier.

The protuberant eyes narrowed slightly at the light coming from the hallway, then he had screwed up his lips like he was tasting something bitter, though Mitch caught a strong whiff of peppermint.

Turning to one side Mitch went on as casually as he could. His back felt exposed. Behind him he suddenly heard the dreadful click. His blood froze and his knees buckled.

Nothing.

He turned round slowly and realized,

rather foolishly, he'd heard the bolt being shot across.

What kind of man sweetens his breath before he visits a whore? he thought, as he crossed the street.

3

OUTSIDE in the street beneath a moonlit velvet sky there were the usual end-of-evening whooping and laughing sounds. A piano tinkled from a saloon and thick, beery voices were raised in some rough harmony. Hodder snaked along in the shadows, only fully exposing himself in the shaft of moonlight between the old adobe buildings that he remembered from the old days as a gunsmith's and a carpenter's. For a second he wondered if he was being followed. He trod more softly and listened for steps but there were none.

He pressed on determinedly, still keeping in the shade. Occasionally a drunk staggered by, or a cowboy with a girl hanging on his neck. This was a night life he knew nothing of. He'd never got into it when a boy, being too young, and he'd no wish now to reduce and weaken himself like these oafs.

He crossed the deserted street and made his way to the livery-stables. It had become his practice last thing whenever he was staying in a town to go and inspect his horse. He slept sounder that way.

He entered the still-open barn of a building from which the dim light of a kerosene lamp was seeping. There was the familiar fruity-sour redolence of animal sweat, leather and hay, piquant with horse piss. His eyes immediately caught sight of the two horses he'd seen earlier outside his hotel. They were in boxes at the far end and next to them was another stallion, a roan, munching hay. Even though they'd been well rubbed down, all three had the dull coats of tired horses.

"Hold it right there!" A gun had been cocked.

He stood stock still, as he'd learnt to do when addressed from behind. *Never turn quickly*, Maguire, an old con, had once told him, *unless you're thinkin' of drawin'. Turn round real nice and slow and smile a big friendly smile.*

Mitch smiled, which was difficult looking down a barrel because his lips seemed somehow paralysed. He opened his palms in innocence and raised his hands. He didn't speak. *Never speak*, Maguire had said. *If they've got yer cornered and are goin' to shoot you they often want you to jabber and plead with 'em before they do it. Don't say nothin' and they'll wait for you to speak. At least you'll gain some time that way.*

The man cocked his trigger.

"You seem pretty interested in them horses," he snapped. He was ruggedly built with a short, thick neck and a pigeon chest. Still Mitch didn't speak. "They shoot horse thieves in these parts."

Mitch was tempted to deny he was a horse thief. But still he remained silent and just stared and smiled at the big, square figure before him; the

32

powerful jaws, the piggy eyes with their expression of aggressive stupidity. He realized his continued smiling was disconcerting the man and he forced his lips still wider and thinner.

If the man had not pointed the pistol at a place just below his navel Mitch might have stayed silent.

"Aw, mister," he said, putting on a stupid hillbilly accent, "Ah work here. Ah'm just messin' out them there hosses."

He'd taken a chance, reckoning on the man not being local. He didn't know for a moment whether it had worked or not because the man stood completely still, appraising him.

"What's your name, boy?"

"Sam, sir," Mitch replied. He sensed the man was a stranger here. "Ah bin lookin' after your hosses real good, mister."

"Whose is that one over there?" said the man, pointing out Mitch's own horse and seeming to be delivering some kind of test.

"That's a stranger's horse sir. He don't b'long round here."

"When did he show up?" The man was staring hard.

"This mornin' just after sun-up sir."

"You don't look like no stable boy. You're not dressed that way."

Mitch smiled again as though pleased at a compliment.

"It's ma evenin' off sir, I been havin' a few beers in town sir, but I allus come in to check the place out on my way home."

At this the granite-faced man started to back out of the stable, his gun still drawn. At the opening he turned out of sight and disappeared. Hodder breathed out sharply and clenched his fists to stop his hands shaking.

Who might that have been? he wondered. Which one of the gang?

He meant to find out.

Advancing to the doorway he listened intently. If the man was still out there Mitch would sense it. Half his blood was Indian and he could hear a man breathing, especially a short-winded slob like the one who'd just left, if he was out there.

Satisfied it was no trick he edged out on to the street and quickly looked both ways. The man was nearly a hundred yards away and just turning left.

Quickly Mitch dashed along the road and up the nearest cross street. He ran to the next gap and looked down yet another street which obviously ran parallel to the main one. Almost immediately he saw the man's solid form go past at the end.

Mitch ran to the next corner, looked round and waited. Half a minute went by but still the man hadn't shown at the other end. He must have stopped somewhere between the two intersections, Mitch reckoned. Perhaps he'd gone into a rooming-house there or turned off down another alley. Mitch jogged to the end and eased himself against the wooden corner. Taking off his hat, he leaned out cautiously. The fat man had disappeared.

It seemed a safe bet that he'd entered the hotel on the other side and Mitch stationed himself in the shadows opposite.

Then, behind the curtain of an upstairs window, he saw the figure curiously foreshortened in the glow of a lamp, like someone seen through the wrong end of a telescope.

He had seen three men tonight and three horses. He would dearly like to have known if there was a fourth. He decided to lurk there and see what might turn up. He had nothing better to do.

★ ★ ★

There were three of them now for sure. In fact there'd been six. Six had been needed for a bank of that size. And six would have gotten clean away and would have been rich men for the rest of their lives but for one thing. They were not prepared to stick it out in their mountain shack for the six weeks that Clem had judged necessary and which, before the robbery, they had agreed on. The sight of the dollars and the gold was too much for them, even for Clem. They decided there was an easier way. If they went off now, burdened with the weight of their ill-gotten gains, they would be sure to be caught or robbed; and if robbed probably killed. No, their best plan was to disperse in different directions, each taking with him enough money to buy a little of the good time — the women, the whiskey, the clothes — that he so desperately wanted, but not so much as to draw attention to himself. Then, any time in the new year, they would make their way down to Jack Hodder's little place in Ashton and he would go and draw their share for them. They knew they could trust Jack, but they each swore to carry out the plan. If one betrayed them in any way, most likely by trying to steal all the gold from Jack, then the rest would band together again and pursue him to the end of time. Otherwise, they'd never meet again, unless by accident in which case they were not to know each other, and they would live happily and very prosperously for the rest of their lives. All this Mitch had been told by his pa, that night when he had come home. It had seemed a good plan. Clem had thought of it, and all his plans had been good ones.

It would have worked as well, except for one thing. Harvey Wharton, always the hot-tempered one, couldn't wait for his money. He'd spent up within a week and almost immediately was knocking on Jack's door, whiskey on his breath, demanding his share.

Mitch had witnessed the scene that followed. His father, obviously surprised and even shocked, had been friendly to the man. They'd slapped each other on the shoulder a bit and made jokes, before sitting down to supper followed by liquor. But then they'd started shouting. He'd heard his father saying,

"It can't be. I've sworn to keep it until after Christmas. We've got to abide by Clem's wishes."

"Like hell!" the burly man had raged. "What's mine is mine and I'm gonna take it now!"

The row seemed to go on all night and Mitch had drifted off to sleep only to be awakened by the sound of a shot. He ran out of his small bedroom at the same time as his mother emerged from hers. They both saw Wharton standing there, the gun smoking in his hand.

At first he seemed paralysed. He jabbered, "It was an accident. I didn't mean to kill him. I were only threatening him. I wanted my money."

The mention of money seemed to galvanize him. "Where is it?" he shouted. "You must know. Come on you Indian bitch, tell me!"

The man took his gun out of his holster once more and trained it on the boy whilst he threatened his mother.

Hodder remembered his mother's

eyes rolling in disbelief, and ignorance, and fear.

Wharton had cocked his trigger but soon there was the sound of galloping hoofs outside as people came to investigate the shot. He made for the door, shouting as he left, "I'll be back. Don't doubt it!"

★ ★ ★

It was two o'clock when Mitch arrived back at his hotel. His vigil had not proved rewarding but he was pleased that he had turned the tables slightly. Now *he* was watching *them*.

He had removed his boots and was on the second landing when he heard men's voices.

"Leave that bottle alone," someone commanded in a loud whisper. "How many times have I told you? We've come too far and lived too long to screw it up now just because you can't leave the filthy stuff alone. Get to bed."

"Aw right, Clem," another voice replied; "tonight'll be my last drinking session until this is all over."

"And for God's sake don't call me Clem! How many times do I have to tell you! I'm known as Luke Allen here. Surely you're not that dumb you can't remember that. There's no point being booked in as Luke Allen here," he seemed to stress the name and repeat it deliberately, "if you're gonna call me something different is there?"

There was no reply.

The same voice went on, "Remember, if we don't use our own names then nothing can tie us with anything that Hodder's kid might say or have said at the trial. Don't forget we've got to be damned careful. People have got longer memories than ya'd believe — especially where there's been a crime. If anything draws attention to us there'll always be somebody to remember us at the trial."

There was a pause and then the sound of snoring.

"The drunken sot," were Mathers' last words.

★ ★ ★

Mitch threw himself wearily on the bed.

The trial. The memory haunted him and would for the rest of his days.

Some months after his pa's death he'd been coming out of the general store when he'd seen Wharton dismounting from a horse and going into the saloon.

The man had worn a moustache and beard but was unmistakable. You could never forget the man who shot your pa.

Straightaway he'd run home for his pa's gun. Not bothering to conceal it, he'd sprinted back and entered the saloon and shot Wharton at point-blank range. The man, however, had taken his gun out like lightning and fired it even while his own eyes were rolling. Mitch had felt himself knocked backwards with a searing pain in his shoulder.

To everyone in the saloon it was clear murder. Everybody said he'd gone loco; it was the Indian blood in him. No one had really liked him in the town because of his being a half-caste, but no one had hated him, either. They'd just treated him different — coldly. Now, however, the local folk would willingly have strung him up. Especially as two strangers came forward to say that Wharton was a respectable man and had been with them out east for the past six months and therefore he couldn't possibly have murdered anyone in Ashton.

At the trial the judge — a fair man, Mitch always thought looking back — seemed to believe the boy had genuinely thought he was revenging his father. From time to time he looked at Wharton's two character witnesses a little dubiously but he had to pronounce the court's verdict of guilty. Mitch never forgot the old grey-haired man's final words; "The court has found you guilty of the crime of murder, but in view of the fact that you are only seventeen and that you have suffered greatly because of the murder of your father, I shall not impose the death penalty but send you to prison for . . . twenty years."

At that there had been booing in the court. "String the Indian up," had been shouted. "Renegade!" "Outcast!" "Half-breed!" "Half-caste!" He heard the taunts as he was led out. As he left he'd made the biggest mistake of his life when, turning to the two strangers who had helped to condemn him, he shouted, "Now you'll never know where it is, will you?"

At the time this had seemed like his revenge on them. Then he could hardly think of twenty years hence and the possibility that they'd still be waiting for him.

4

H E was up early and out on the street; he had things to do.

First he went to the general store and bought provisions and more cartridges. Next he went to the livery-stables again, checked on his horse and theirs, paid for five more nights and filled his saddle-bags. He could now pull out at a moment's notice, if it was necessary.

He was ready. As ready as he'd ever be — but ready for what? Ready to move when he had to, he guessed.

He chewed over what would happen if the gang saw him heading out. Would they follow him as close as his shadow or would they give him a head start like they had been doing?

Would they in fact be able to follow him close enough to stop him getting the gold, especially if he went in the dark using his Indian stealth? It would certainly not be easy for them, but he had long ago come to realize that, where big money is concerned, anything is possible.

These men had been waiting twenty years for this moment. They'd spent a small fortune following him this far. They would stop at nothing now. They'd gone too far down the trail. By now they must be getting impatient; desperate, even. That might work in his favour. Or it might not. They might kill him rashly. But then, he figured, the one rash act they couldn't risk was to kill him now. They'd made that mistake with his pa. If there was going to be any killing it would be after they'd got what they wanted. Everything pointed to the fact that he should stay well away from the gold, act like he'd come back to his home-town to settle down and start again; play dumb; act like he'd never even heard of the gold.

Equally he knew he couldn't do

that, not even to frustrate and thwart his enemies. He couldn't because he was impatient, too. He'd waited just as long as them and with an even greater smouldering sense of injustice and gnawing hunger for revenge. They were only motivated by greed.

But the real reason it had to be now was that it was pointless to delay. It had got to be him or them, sometime. Because even if he succeeded in getting away with the gold today, they would still be there on his tail tomorrow.

Call it intuition or whatever, he knew that the next few days would provide a bloody outcome to the story that had begun in Bucksville half a lifetime ago. The time had come.

★ ★ ★

A man in Mitch's position will show an interest in anything and everything that passes him by. He becomes just plain old-fashioned nosy because his life might depend on it.

47

He was crossing the main street and intending to go down to his hotel when in the distance he saw a white post-chaise. It was by no means the usual sort of inelegant vehicle seen out West and he felt drawn to look it over. He quickened his pace till he reached it and then slowed to saunter by.

Seated in it was a woman, resplendent in a white hat and high-collared dress, who plainly took considerable care over her appearance. The last time he'd seen her she'd been a coltish young girl with her hair flowing like a torrent on to bare shoulders. It could still have set fire to a bale of straw at twenty paces but it was now arranged in short, delicate curls.

They say a woman never forgets the man — in her case the boy — who takes away her maidenhood. But she didn't know him. She didn't even notice him. Her eye passed over him without a flicker of recognition.

She was bored, preoccupied, lounging in the back of the carriage, with two heavy-jawed cowboys in front. In the instant he saw her his heart gave up the illusion of love it might once have felt.

Time had hardened her just like it had hardened the tart, Maisie. There was something in her that was remote. Her head was turned sideways and her lips were slightly parted, revealing the perfect, dazzling teeth of old. But there was no warmth in that mouth any more and there was indifference in her eyes, indifference to all things.

All that youthful, breathless gaiety had gone from a face which had once never been still. It was in truth hardly changed; it was perhaps a little less round, more beautiful even, but there was nothing in it. It was no longer animated; it was as though she were asleep with open eyes.

He tried to read her countenance for a hint of tragedy or just a shadow of disappointment. But he couldn't. Her beautiful face was just a blank, betraying nothing, neither happiness nor sadness.

"Jenny," he said softly.

He had not meant to speak.

She turned, surprised to be addressed. The two men turned and gave him up-and-down stares. They looked at her for direction but she motioned them to stare away with a wave of her hand.

She was baffled. Still she had not recognized him. Then there was that smile, like the first glow of dawn after a stormy night.

"Mitch!" She pressed a hand to her lips. "It can't be you. *Is* it you?"

She had extracted a smile from him but he could not conceal the sadness in his eyes.

"Yeh, it's me."

She stood up and with a sinuous grace started to step down from the carriage. He helped her down, for a second holding her gloved hand in his.

"Let me look at you," she said.

He swept off his hat and ran his fingers through his sleek hair. "Am I that changed?" he asked.

She appraised him, almost but not quite affectionately. After a while she spoke. "What do you want, Mitch?"

She had answered with a question and had stopped smiling. It took him aback.

"I've come home."

"Home!" she repeated, incredulously.

"It's good to see you, Jenny," he heard himself saying.

A throat cleared.

A man was leaning on the rail on the porch in front of the bank.

"And it's good to see you again, Mitch."

He was dressed in black. His hat, set at a rakish angle, was of the same colour as his black double-breasted shirt, ornately snaked on the lapels with gold filigree.

He was enjoying the joke of knowing Mitch but not being known to him — or so he imagined.

Mitch never forgot a face. When last he'd seen this one it had belonged to a boy as slender as a bull-whip and with a thatch of yellow hair. He could not now be much more than thirty-four or five but he looked older. His body had coarsened and stiffened and his eyes were sunken darkly, contrasting with his pallid skin. He was smoking a black cheroot.

"My husband," murmured Jenny.

"Jed Bellow," remarked Mitch without surprise.

"Yeh, that's me." The man seemed no longer amused. His voice was thin and hard. "What took you so long to get home, boy?"

"We heard you got released over a year ago," said Jenny.

"I was in no hurry," said Mitch sombrely. He resented being 'boyed' by the younger man. "I didn't want to come back all skin and bone."

Bellow forced a laugh and stepped down to street level. Mitch noticed he was not tall, despite the over-sized heels of his shining walnut-coloured boots.

"You plannin' on stayin' long?"

The two men seemed to have come face to face. Mitch got the feeling that on these terms he would win any exchange.

"Maybe!" he said.

Jed's eyes jerked a get-in-the-carriage look to his wife. He climbed in after her, gave the driver a double pat on the shoulder and a gee-up click of the teeth.

"Well boy, you sure come an' see me," he said, "and we'll see what we can do to fix you up with a job." The wheels had started to move. "Now don't forget now."

Mitch watched the disappearing carriage, the matched pair of brown horses, the three dark stetsons and the lady's white hat. She had not turned round.

★ ★ ★

The temptation to grab the gold and run was almost irresistible. The waiting was the worse because he had nothing to wait for. Except their first move.

The eating house he selected was old and dilapidated, seemingly out of step with the rest of the town but more in tune with his own mood. The boards of the porch creaked under his weight as he strolled with a slow, loose, casual stride past the gawking pawky faces of three old men who lounged there. He smiled tightly at them. It was facetious only to those who wished to take it as such. The pleasantly inclined could easily have taken it as a friendly greeting.

Inside, more men were smoking, drinking coffee, or eating. Their bloated faces froze as Mitch entered and the hush was deep and menacing. They looked hate, a strange hate with a loathsome joy in it. They were flabby, crabby men who spent the heat of the afternoon indoors, happy in their grudging.

The spleen on their faces said they knew him all right.

"What can I get you, boy?"

It was a tall and stringy woman speaking; she was no advert for good eating.

"We don't have no Indians in here," another voice rapped out from behind. Mitch turned round slowly to face it and advanced on a florid man who he figured for the speaker.

"I would advise you to leave now, friend," he said in a low tone. "Stay and die if you have a mind to."

There was a moment of hot and empty silence. The perspiration gathered on the man's brows as he stuck out his chin pugnaciously and rounded in his lips about to speak defiance. Suddenly the chair scraped; he stood up and reeled out, having thought better of it.

"Everything, ma'am," said Mitch to the woman.

Which turned out to be an immense platter of fried chicken, enveloped with dumplings, a slice of bacon and a sunny-side egg.

Even whilst he was devouring it

the woman returned with a heaped-up dish of potatoes. He washed the lot down with hot coffee, drunk from a thrice-refilled, battered tin mug, and sweetened with dark molasses.

Still the smoke-filled room was silent; all eyes were on him, glazed and unblinking. It was as though his presence carried some invisible force, stifling all animation.

He tipped back his hat and continued to drink the dark brew under their gazes. It didn't bother him. For once in his life he found it easy to act with assurance. It required no effort to let it be known he was unmoved and unshaken and, most of all, unbowed. It came so easy because it pained them so much.

It was the look in his eyes which was getting through to them — the pride that it showed, the fact that it gave no hint of remorse for his crime, whether that was murder or, maybe worse, having mixed blood. He was the prodigal come home but without the big show of success that would secure the welcome, wipe out the past and, miraculously, even lighten his skin.

Suddenly he gave an old gap-toothed cragface an enormous wink and then smiled winningly — in a mocking sort of way — at all of them. In fact, he was fighting back the compulsion to laugh in contempt at these men who had nothing better to do than silently hate.

The more they glowered, the more he smiled. And the more he smiled, the more he managed to show he didn't give a shit for them.

"You're not eating," he said, looking at all of them. "You're not drinking." They didn't reply. "Now don't let me put you good neighbours off. Don't let no poor half-caste bum . . . no-good Injun keep you god-fearin' men from your sweet, old-fashioned jawbonin'."

One by one they were shuffling out. He didn't know why he was bothering to do this, forcing his smile even wider. What did he hope to gain?

It was just that there was no other way. People like this fed on their hate and anger. Let them have plenty to go at. Let them see him back in Ashton as large as life. They were going to see him anyway and to talk about him so he might as well give them something to chew on.

He figured he'd be more likely to be left alone that way. If the bastards sensed weakness in him, he'd be hounded. This way he just maybe might not have to draw his gun. It was a big maybe.

His smile had turned malicious. He wiped his mouth, stood up and went out.

★ ★ ★

He had been in his room no more than the time it took to splash some water on his face when he heard the heavy clomp on the stairs. He tautened a little but not much because men who mean to kill go silent.

58

The door was thumped and a raucous voice shouted, "Open up, Hodder."

"Who is it?"

"Sheriff Tex Brownlee."

He drew his gun and, without moving in front of the door, slid back the bolt and called the man to enter. A mountain came in real slow and blocked the doorway. He was craggy-faced, granite-jawed, with a quantity of grey hair in his nose and ears. Maybe a handful of years older than Mitch, he was a half-a-foot bigger; and he was, indeed, sporting a badge. Contemptuously he looked at Mitch's iron.

"You better put that away, Indian." He spat out some tobacco juice. "Unless yer figurin' on usin' it." He spat again, a great filthy glob.

As Mitch holstered his Colt, he judged there was a look of hatred and recklessness in this man. Here was someone who would not have second thoughts about killing him.

"Word round here, Indian, is that

you killed a man in cold blood."

"The man murdered my pa."

"Bull! The man had never been hereabouts afore."

"Who told you that?"

"I heard, sonny. It's part of my job to know these things. When a murderer comes in my town I find out."

"Call me a murderer if you want — but I've done my time. I'm a free man. If I did wrong I sure was punished for it . . . for twenty years."

"Twenty years dunt mean nothin' set against the life of a man you gunned down, mister."

Mitch could see the conversation was going to go round in circles. The sheriff would come out with the same argument if Mitch spoke against the man he'd killed.

"What can I do for you, Sheriff?" His tone was firm but polite.

"You can get the hell out of here by sundown."

"This is my home-town."

"Like hell! We don't have no bums

60

here. This is a respectable town now. It's a good law-abidin' place; we don't have no vermin like you, Hodder. Everythin's changed. Get that!"

The man sat on a chair, leaned back, hands behind his head, and hooked his spurs onto the bedhead.

"I ain't leavin' yet awhile, Sheriff, not until I've finished my business here."

The huge man stood up furiously and moved so close Mitch caught the reek of whiskey on his breath.

"You leave, sonny, when I tell you. You've got no — I repeat *no* — business here. No one does business here with a bum like you. Get back in your saddle, boy, and git — if you know what's good for you."

"Jed Bellow's a personal friend of mine. He's big business here and he's gonna give me a job."

Mitch smiled cockily, as provocatively as he could. He knew that, as unlikely as this story might appear to the lawman, he would at least back off at this point until he'd checked — unless of course Bellow had sent him.

"As it happens, Bellow's a personal friend of mine, too," snapped the sheriff, "and I happen to know he don't hold you in high esteem."

Mitch thinned his lips wryly. He had his answer. In a way it pleased him to conclude that Brownlee was in Bellow's pay. Because it had crossed his mind that it could be the gang that he was in cahoots with. There would be nothing more likely to drive him to the gold than being run out of town. But he figured Mathers would be too cagey to advertise himself to the sheriff; and certainly not stupid enough to do business with a man who could easily double-cross him. Brownlee looked like a man who'd double-cross his own mother, if he'd ever had one.

"By dusk, Hodder," the sheriff was saying, "you be gone. You be far away." He slapped his holster meaningfully. "And if you figure on trying it wi' me, boy, you'll find there ain't nobody quicker on the draw and no better shot than me in these parts. Plenty have tried it . . . "

The door slammed.

* * *

He pulled across the dark curtains and sank down into the uncomfortable wooden chair. He did not doubt his own courage or his reactions. His rawboned hand zipped his gun out, twirled it and then reholstered it, all in one rippling action.

He'd perfected that in prison, under Maguire's joyless instruction with a lump of wood stuck in his pants pocket.

Concentrate on speed, just whipping the thing out in one blur, the old man had said.

What's the use o' this, Mitch had moaned. What in tarnation's the good of being quick on the draw if I never get to shoot nuthin'? I can't practise without I get to aim and fire a real gun at summ'n.

You don't aim a Colt, boy! Maguire had been incensed. *You point it and trigger it. It'll do the rest.*

So day after day the practice had gone on, Mitch aware that one day his life would surely depend on it. Because always Maguire would be drumming one message into him; when a man packs a gun he's making himself a target; he must be able and ready to use it.

Almost Mitch's first action when getting out was to strap on a Colt and draw it with the speed of lightning. That had been one hell of a moment, his blood running hot and feverish.

He went downstairs and banged on the counter. The weasel-faced one appeared. Seeing him standing for the first time, Mitch realized how small he was, before he hauled himself up on to his chair and squatted there, his face level with Mitch's.

"I want," said Mitch slowly, "the key

to the room beneath mine that the two drifters are in."

"That's impossible!"

Mitch gave him an amused, reflective expression. He put out his hand. The man was doing his durndest to stop his own from shaking.

"Nothin's impossible, friend," said Mitch. "Fur instance, it's not impossible that you'll be dead within a minute, carried out in the next five, buried tomorra and forgotten the day after." His tone was full of sad reasonableness. "We all do dumb things from time to time, friend, but you surely ain't gonna do one now. You surely ain't about to die just to stop me seein' a little ol' room — cos I'm gonna see it anyway . . . "

The key appeared. This time the man dropped it quickly into the outstretched palm and snatched back his hand, fearful it might be crushed again.

Mitch smiled. "Thanks, friend."

The room was virtually a replica of his own, except in that addition to the big bed it had a pallet in the corner.

He searched everywhere thoroughly but found nothing of interest. He didn't expect to. The men up against him were professionals who travelled light. His chief purpose had been to establish to the hotel clerk, and therefore to the sheriff, a connection between himself and the two cowboys. Let *them* have a visitation.

He returned to his own room, quickly sinking into a brooding depression, aware of the limits of his options. He'd just worked off a little of his anger on the clerk and accomplished next to nothing. There was nothing he could do now except wait.

As soon as he lay down on the bed he felt a stirring deep and unsettlingly within him. It made him sweat. It made him get up and pace the room.

It was not anger precisely, although that was part of it. He did not know precisely what it was. Precision, if it exists in any form, was not at this time in great supply out west, nor is it to be found in human emotion anywhere. He felt himself to be crowded, re-living again the memory of grey confinement. He had merely exchanged one prison for another.

★ ★ ★

This time he would enjoy her. It would not just be staccato and functional. That part of it, indeed, was over and done with at almost the first blasting. And then he made love to her, like a woman with flame hair had taught him to make love to *her*, proudly, teasingly, tenderly, cruelly.

"Maisie," he whispered. There was enquiry and pleading and urgency in his voice. "Do something for me."

She said nothing; he pounded punishingly.

"Maisie!"

His voice was louder, more strident. He pounded again until she bit her lip with pain.

Finally she asked him what he wanted.

"Moan," he said and thrust again, occupying every inch of her.

He felt he was battering at a shell, trying to destroy it and find the shy stranger waiting to be wooed. She, at first merely professionally accommodating, began by degrees to respond to his steady pounding. But it was when he occasionally broke rhythm and pounded deliberately on the off-beat that he knew he was getting to her. This seemed to awaken excitement in her, especially when it was followed up with a greater double pounding. Her pelvis had started to shift and her breathing was coming heavy.

It was when he became gentle once more, caressing and kind of twisting as he thrust that she began to do as he commanded. She whimpered. Instantly he became cruel again, bludgeoning and thudding with his body weight, and she moaned.

It was, he realized, his rapid changes

that awoke her unfaked interest and when he found her moving to pleasure he pulled away. Then he was with her again, mastering her, pounding, hammering once more, then gently thrusting. He squeezed her breasts, drawing his thumb across the nipple he had persuaded to erectness, whilst his middle finger supported it from below. Then when he pounded again, she screamed with pleasure and convulsed explosively.

She opened her eyes; to him they were no longer those of a whore, indifferent, workaday. She had been caught up in something she didn't understand, and which she had never known, or had long ago forgotten if indeed she had ever known it. Whilst he remained inside her she squeezed her thighs round him, vicing him back to vitality.

Later, much later, she opened her eyes once more and sighed. "Hey — gee," she said, "I'm the one who's supposed to know all the tricks."

"I'm gonna take you out to supper some night," he said, caressing the long black hair which hung about her shoulders and lustred in the candlelight. "Somewhere away from here. With bright lights and faces. Faces that don't curl up. I'll dress you in blue velvet and we'll drink champagne out of your silver slipper."

She smiled to herself intently. Then her mouth compressed to a button. Her eyes were wild and staring — mad. They were riveted on his face, her high-cheekboned features fixed and sour.

"Go," she said. "Go and don't come back! I'm doin' the best a girl can round here." Her voice was dry and cracked. "People will always look down on an Indian and a tart."

The stark reference to his blood sobered him. He had lost all his momentary verve.

"I was kidding," he said, and left.

5

IT was full dark when he stepped out into the street and headed in the direction of his hotel. One thing about Clem Mathers, he thought, the low-down son-of-a — certainly knows how to watch a man without making it obvious.

Unlike last night there was no one around; strange in a town as busy as this and with the hour still quite early. He cursed himself for having come out, lured into danger by the need for a woman. The silence echoing and rebounding all around was not right, not natural.

That tightening in his gut again. The warning it gave he knew was always for real.

He had to descend from the boardwalk at the front of a narrow, dead-black alley. He hesitated before crossing. An owl soughed low overhead, alarming him momentarily. The alley had no sound, no movement.

He hurried across and breathed a sigh of relief as he reached the other side and pressed himself hard against a wall black and solid in the night's soft darkness.

Then somewhere out there something clicked; nothing more than that but Mitch felt himself drawn and tight, his nerves cocked and hair-triggered. He crouched low to make himself a smaller target and listened, still as a dead thing in the shadows, his gun drawn.

He wanted badly to relax, to stand up and stroll away. But something — the instinct for self-preservation — was telling him not to.

He was powerless, unable to move, skewered to the spot by his fears.

Suddenly a thunderclap sent a draft past his cheek and clanged behind him. Another shot slammed out as he twisted and dived to street level, rolling over and returning fire as he sprang in one spasm.

He ran crazily, ducking and half-stumbling as shot after shot detonated around him.

He flung himself round a corner, fired off three more rounds into the darkness and felt himself lurching against the wall. It was then that he realized he'd been hurt. Blood was oozing from his side and a sudden pain had started throbbing.

Behind him the shooting had stopped and the night was as eerily quiet as it had been. The whole thing had been a matter of seconds, the time it takes for a man to die.

He was hardly a longer time in the livery-stables, throwing on his saddle-bags and bed-roll.

He got off Main Street at a gallop; the risk was less that way. The quicker he moved, he figured, the less likely would the next bullet aimed at his back find its target.

It was as if someone, the gods for instance, had suddenly run out of patience and everything had speeded up in consequence.

* * *

He found himself banging at a door to which memory had directed him. Now it had a brass plate on it, not seen on his last visit, but the name of the occupant had not changed. This raised his spirits but he felt them sinking fast as the knocking brought no response, not even the flutter of a curtain or scrape of a footstep.

In desperation he called out, "Doc, are you in there? This is Mitch Hodder and I'm hurt real bad. You remember me, Doc, I'm Jack Hodder's son."

The words seemed to echo round forlornly in the night's stillness. He swallowed his own black bile, as he cursed the doctor for not opening up and cursed himself for calling out his own name. Doc Turnbull sure owed his pa plenty. Some might say he owed him everything since his pa had saved his life when they were both on the trail years back. That was in the days Doc Turnbull was better known as a barber than a medical man.

But men have short memories. If Doc remembered an obligation at all maybe he thought he'd discharged it when pulling the slug out of Mitch's shoulder that time.

Just as Mitch, holding his side beneath the luridly mottled shirt, was about to walk away, he heard bolts being shot back.

A small, frail old man stood there in shirt sleeves. The hair was now a mere grey stubble but the eyes were the same shrewd watery-grey.

They held him fiercely in their stare. So long was their examination of him, in fact so leisured and clinical, that the doctor had an almost supernatural knowledge of him, to which his heavy breathing and doubled-up posture only contributed greater strength.

"Come in," he said in a whisper. "When I heard you were back I wondered how many days it would be before I was operating on yer."

Still grumbling to himself he led the way into his surgery and lit the kerosene lamp with a disturbingly shaky hand.

"Take yer shirt off and lay down here," he snapped, pointing to the sort of scrubbed wooden table most commonly seen in butchers. It had last borne Mitch's weight some twenty years back when the speaker had been steady-handed, dark-haired and fortyish.

Doc Turnbull walked across to a wash-stand, poured water into a bowl and started to scrub up. As he did so his wife entered carrying a cauldron; steaming water was slopping out of it as she walked.

"You're lucky boy," said the doctor. "Two inches higher and it would have pierced your lung."

He had a towel on the wound absorbing the blood. Then, as far as Mitch could see, he seemed to stick a swab into the hole in his side. The pain was intense.

"Bite on this," he was told. Something was thrust between his teeth.

The doctor removed the swab and gently poured on the disinfecting alcohol. Mitch convulsed in agony, his eyes screwed tight.

"Sssh," came the soothing voice of the woman. "That'll stop you getting an infection. You're lucky, not many doctors use it."

Mitch opened his eyes only briefly to see the doctor holding a probe by a pair of tongs. It felt red-hot when it entered his flesh. It was jabbing him, needling into him, goading, going deeper and deeper.

"Scream if you want to," the doctor said casually. "They mostly do."

Mitch drifted in and out of consciousness. He heard a quiet request for forceps on one occasion. Then he felt a tugging at his innards. Later, much later, he heard a 'ping'.

It was the red bullet being cast into a metal dish. The doctor seemed to be examining it with interest whilst his wife continued the swabbing.

After she'd applied some cooling ointment she put a pad on his wound and gently started to wrap a long cummerbund of a bandage round his middle. Every time he had to arch his back to let the bandage through he was lanced with pain.

Grim-faced, the doctor would accept no payment. There was no emotion in him. He seemed neither pleased nor displeased to have seen Mitch. His wife had disappeared as discreetly as she had arrived. It was all over; Mitch was patched up and leaving.

All doc said as he closed the door was, "I'll be seeing you again, young man, no doubt."

Mitch hauled himself into the saddle and smiled, thinly, a sad smile but which, as it twisted into a snarl, contained a strange joy. He had survived.

Then he moved off, slouching un-Indianlike with stooping shoulders.

What a town, he thought.

6

THE cowboy rode the dim, lonely trail, every dusty inch of which he'd once known like the back of his hand. He remembered so well the dry scent of the night wind through the scrub. He was going home. Given the awful and inexorable march of events he had to.

It didn't make sense. It was crazy. Why should Mathers have wanted him killed? He was only valuable to them alive. He was their meal-ticket. But there was no doubt about it; someone had been out for his blood.

It crossed his mind that perhaps they had been shooting to miss. Just trying to frighten him. But that seemed way out. Gunfire in the dark is a dangerous business. No one can guarantee either to hit or miss a moving target. And he had a strong feeling they had been mighty close to killing him.

After a while he reined in his horse, listening for the sound of hoofs. But no one was following.

The more he thought about events, the more he was puzzled. No, nothing made sense. The whole strategy of the gang had been to make him think he was out on his own. They wanted him to lead them straight to the money, not to be frightened away from Ashton. If nothing else the actions of tonight would certainly stir things up around the place and have the sheriff gunning for him even more determinedly.

Once more he looked back down the trail. Once his eyes had been able to spear through the darkness like a cat's. He had lost that. But in a way, his hearing, always acute, seemed more developed. No, he was not being followed. Which meant that he could go to ground for as long as his provisions held out. Or as long as he could control his other appetites.

Having broken his way in with three

lusty kicks to the door, he struck match after match, filling the room with the acrid smell of burning sulphur, momentarily masking the stench of decay and neglect that had pervaded. For a second he was overcome by one old and still-familiar item. Everything else had been ripped out and looted but the old stone sink, with the pump-handle to pull up water from the tank outside, remained. It was part of his boyhood. It reminded him of summer days when parched from being out all day he would run in and work the handle.

It was here in winter he would huddle next to his ma for warmth. His pa was almost always away. She would tell him wild, weird Indian tales . . .

He drifted away and, on the rough floor, slept the sleep of those grey years that followed, those grey interminable years that dragged on just like the grey men slogging it out on the chain-gang . . .

He watched the sorrel pony picking its way down the steep, winding track.

She slid out of the saddle, holding down her long, thin skirt, and strolled towards him. She had come to a meeting which had been twenty years deferred. She was, however, a different person, someone serene of manner and carrying herself elegantly. It was an elegance enhanced by the inches she had added.

He was lying on the ground, propped up on an elbow. He wondered for a second if Jenny would sit down beside him, but he sensed that the girl who would once so willingly have reclined had become proudly and haughtily upright.

He noticed again the absence of freckles and the paleness of her face, arms and legs. She was wearing a full-brimmed round hat with tiny pink flowers clustered on it.

She hesitated for a moment and then spoke. "I can only stay a minute. I daren't be away longer."

Her lips compressed and she looked away. He had given her a look which once would have chastened her and then melted her, but not now.

"If I give you some money," she said, still looking away, "all the money I can raise, will you go? For your own safety's sake?" He merely arched his eyebrows, in contempt of her offer. "Look, you're hungry, you've no money, you look like a saddle-tramp! Take my money and go." She held out a purse.

"Your money!"

"Well, all right, Jed's money. Take it and go. You can't stay here, it's a changed town. Jed owns everything and he's a jealous man. He knows about us way-back. Sometimes he gets insanely jealous because . . . he didn't marry a virgin. He'd kill you now if he thought I'd been to see you."

"It was him who had me ambushed last night?"

She looked shocked, almost on the point of breaking down. But she clung on to her dignity. "I don't know anything about that. But I know he'll not accept you in this town."

Mitch raised himself to his feet and this seemed to alarm her. She started to edge backwards.

"How did he get so mighty rich and powerful if a poor saddle-bum like me might make so bold as to enquire, ma'am?" he asked savagely.

"Deals in property. Speculation. Getting in at the right time."

She had spoken too quickly.

"But who staked him in the first place? Seems to me he were the son of a nobody when I was around these parts."

"When his pa died he sold the shop. He made a good bit from that, then he went out east and came back with more. He was rich when he came back."

"What did he come back for?"

Her head hung. "For me," she said almost inaudibly.

"You knew him before, then?"

"Yes."

"You can't have wasted much time after I left!"

"Mitch," it was the first time she'd used his name "you can't possibly have expected a girl of just seventeen to wait for you, to waste her life, her childbearing years, waiting for a man who's in prison — who might or might not come back." It came out all in one breath, like a speech she knew by heart.

He stood very still, looking down at the ground. The conversation had dwindled away now that she had said her piece.

His jaw set firm, he looked her straight in the eye as he refused the purse she was holding out again.

"T'ain't right for a woman to be staking a man," he said in a low tone. "But that's not the real reason. I ain't leavin'."

She shrugged, turned away, mounted, deftly kneed the pony and was away, halfway up the hill before he came out of a sort of daze. He wanted to call her back, but he watched her go with a still, set expression.

After a long while of staring at the top of the hill where she'd vanished he doggedly began the climb.

At the top there was a light and soothing breeze. The peachy sky was suffused with wispy golden cirrus and the line of the horizon was hazy in places. This was good, rich, and beautiful country, which unrolled beneath him.

He couldn't wait to see the back of it.

Much later he went down to the little pool which had always been two or three feet deep, except in the driest of seasons when the underground spring which fed it became a shy bubbling.

Except for his hat, in the crown of which he balanced his Colt, he was naked as he waded out to cleanse himself. He lathered all over, except the area of his wound, with a bar of yellow carbolic, and watched the soapy scum floating away. He made waves with his feet to bring up clear water which he dabbed around his wound.

There was no need to dry off in the warm breeze and within a few minutes he was dressed and strolling back to the sound of a sniggering mockingbird.

The sun was westering now, bathing the rugged range of hills in a golden light that merged into a crimson glow. Dark shadows gathered at their feet. It was the quiet end of the day, the thinking time.

He hunkered down to take some of the pressure off his wound, watching the shadows lengthen, deep in thought. The fact that he'd been shot seemed to have put it all in perspective. He could so easily have died.

He could still slip away and disappear into the mountains. There was no absolute compulsion on him to bring it all to a show-down now. And yet matters seemed to have gone too far for him to ride out.

The peace and stillness here was unreal. It belonged to a different part of his life, a time of innocence long past. He knew what he was facing, although he had no plan of campaign. But he sensed that this place where he was born was where he must make his stand.

He started to put together the wood for a small fire which he would light as soon as the purple now descending had turned black. The eerie silence seemed to grow thin with the shadows. But as night settled it brought its soft sounds, as though magnified to the ear as the visual faded; the silver slur of water in the creek and the faintest stir of air as a night-hawk dipped.

The hills were now harshly defined, a serrated line of darkest olive, as he lit the match and heard the fire crackle to life. Sparks leapt as the flames embraced each other.

For some reason, though the night was still warm the fire made him shiver. He stood up and caught the frail lights of Ashton in the distance. One of them no doubt would be the red lantern where would be Maisie and all her warmth, her beauty and the tenderness which only he could evoke.

He thought of the huge bed, the mound of soft pillows, the silky sheets, the excitement he'd seen in her eyes. His hands were stroking her. He was caressing her, his mouth at her nipple, his hands massaging her thigh.

She was moaning.

He stared at the lights a long time and then busied himself bringing out food from the shack. He brought his coffee to the boil and supped the aromatic brew in silence while waiting for the beans to heat and the bacon to crisp in the skillet. When he was all through he kicked dust over the fire to kill the smouldering.

In half-an-hour he could be with Maisie. The thoughts of so much pleasure, at a distance but so near, kept recurring as he sought sleep, filling him with the intoxicating and aching consciousness of his intended act.

7

HE woke up early, soaked in sweat, and peeped out of the narrow gap between the boards at the window. His eyes gazed on a shimmering morning. On the right the hills merged with the sky in a sunny haze.

Then he saw the stain of dust rising and advancing, like the plume from a railroad engine. There was a whole bunch of fast-moving riders down the track.

They were heading out here to the point and they were coming to see him — at a hell of a pace!

He checked his Colt, spinning the barrel round. It was a well-oiled machine, deadly in a one-to-one encounter. But just about useless against the number of men who were kicking up such a dust.

It was just possible that they were riding out some place. After all, who knew he was here? No one had followed him. Only Jenny had guessed it. Maybe she'd been followed. Or maybe she'd just said.

There was nothing to give him away. His horse was well hidden. He knew he was clinging to false hopes. He knew they were coming to finish off what they'd started in Ashton. They'd missed him there, but today the odds were even more heavily with them. He was penned in. There'd be no shadows to hide him.

He did not have long to wait — five minutes, maybe six, and they were near enough for him to count them. Twelve riders; so they reckoned they needed a dozen to take him. If every one of his bullets found its target, he would only have to reload once.

At the front was a big man, head and shoulders above the rest. It had to be the sheriff.

One minute more and the shack was

surrounded. It had all looked like a well-planned operation. The men had dismounted, fanned out and circled round, each having found himself a sizeable chunk of rock for protection.

Yeh, they meant business this time all right. The best he could hope for was to take a few with him when they eventually had to rush him. He would die in the house where he was born — where his pa and ma had died. Maybe someone would put yellow flowers on his grave — if he was given one.

"Come out, Hodder!" It was Brownlee's voice. "We'll give you ten seconds before we torch the place."

An eerie silence.

"Come out, Hodder, with yer hands up!" It was the same rasping voice. "Come out unless you want to fry."

He stood up from his crouching position, kicked open the door, went out real slow. *When a gun's on ya, never make a sudden movement*, Macguire had said. *Never do anything to help them pull the trigger.*

He walked with his head held high, his arms above his head, blinking away the blinding sweat.

He was surrounded, kicked, cuffed, rabbit-punched. They were mean men who enjoyed the mean business.

He was being half-carried, half-dragged towards the tree opposite his house. The one he used to swing on as a boy. His hat was torn off and a rope was being put over his head. His feet were being bound.

"Yer gonna die, Hodder. Yer gonna swing, boy. I told you to git outta town but you're still here. Now why might that be?"

Mitch might have replied. He might have said that he was in his own house. He might have spat in the sheriff's eye. He might have, if the rope hadn't been throttling him.

Brownlee was shouting. It was all words. "Injun . . . Ashton . . . scum . . . vermin . . . half-caste, told you to get outta town . . ."

He was being lifted on to a horse; the rope was tightening. He seemed to be incredibly high, and rising. His life was passing before him. His birth, his unhappy youth, his young manhood when the primitive in him had driven him to revenge and put him forever on the wrong side of the law. His brain was boiling. He was choking. The horse slipped from under him.

He felt the drop. Then all went black.

* * *

Water was being squeezed into his mouth. He was gasping for breath, his throat burning inside and out. A soft hand was massaging the back of his neck.

A woman bent over him but all he could see at first was her smooth, round bosom and a cascade of red hair.

He was dead. He had to be. Was this, then, a ministering angel? His eyes met hers. They were large and dark and looking down at him with tenderness and pity but they lacked their customary lustre and the skin underneath them looked as though she had been weeping or had gone without sleep. He could hear her breath and feel it cool on his face. He put his arm round her waist. It was flesh and blood all right. Not the heavenly ether of an angel. He felt her start and then begin to tremble.

"Jenny," he croaked. "What . . . happened?"

The pain of speaking was excruciating.

"Sssh!" she said, soothingly. "Don't speak."

He tried to sit upright but she held him down with gentle pressure.

"Did you cut me down?" he said.

"No, I got here too late. Somebody had already done it. Brownlee, I reckon."

"Brownlee!" Of all the men to cut him down he'd be the last. "Not Brownlee!"

"He didn't want to kill you. I heard him talking to my husband last night. Bellow said he wanted you dead. Brownlee said if you went for your gun he'd kill you. Otherwise he couldn't. There'd be too many witnesses and he wasn't about to step outside the law."

He sat up slowly. It was as though somebody was driving a stake into the nape of his neck.

"I ran in and pleaded for you. I told Jed he and I were all through if he could think of murdering a man in cold blood. I said, what has Mitch ever done to you? But he just . . . "

"What?"

"It's hard to say. A look came over him like . . . " She shuddered. "I can't describe it. It was like he was mad. It was horrible."

He dragged himself to his feet. "So it was Brownlee I have to thank for my life. He just wanted to scare mc off."

His arms went round her waist again. This time she did not resist. It was an awkward embrace, she taking most of his weight.

"He'd have killed you all right if he could have made it look legal."

He started to kiss her slowly and gently, the longing of years ebbing out. His strong gentle fingers contoured her breasts. He felt a wild desire spring up and a hard urgency.

"Mitch," she shrieked, "I'll never see you again." She broke away and ran towards the sorrel. "You gotta leave town now. Never come back. It's 'cos of me he wants you dead. He's just about as jealous as any man can be."

She leaned down and kissed him softly on the forehead. Crystal tears were running down her cheeks. Then she was gone again, for ever.

There was a new feeling in him now, a kind of rage welling up from deep inside him. Twenty years in prison, interminable years where each day seemed a thousand, had been only the prelude to an even greater form of hell. He began to wonder if he could die. Had the two brushes with death merely proved the gods were merciless? He had not been marked out for gentle oblivion but for a life of torture and oppression.

He spat blood from his mouth. He would beat the bastards, whoever they were, by sheer force of will.

8

THE old crone let him in tonight without a nod, her mouth clamtight.

He took the steps lightly, two at a time. His second brush with death seemed to have increased his appetite for life even more than the first. Maisie looked stunned as she opened the door.

"I didn't expect you; I heard you'd left town a couple of days ago," was all she said, but she seemed to be putting undue emphasis on her words. He wondered if that was a gesture of impatience she made with her eyes as he started to unbuckle. She edged away from him, watching intently as he laid the gunbelt on the dresser.

"I've come to say goodbye," he said.

He advanced towards her, smiling,

and pushed her down on the bed. His fingers dawdled through her hair and he removed the silver headband, letting the rich tresses free. He started to nuzzle the soft, downy flesh at the nape of her neck, biting it softly.

His arms moved down her bodice, slowly over the contours of her hips and coming to rest on her thighs. His warm breath caressed her skin like feathers. His voice was husky and he seemed to speak into her mouth. "What's wrong?"

She was stiff; her eyes were open but unfocused as though she did not want to see something but dare not blot it out.

Why did he have to go through this agony of rejection tonight of all nights? he wondered. He had expected it sometime but why now when he was leaving? What had brought it on? What had he done to deserve it?

Then he heard it. Once more the cocking of the trigger. He ought to be getting used to it by now. He froze and dwindled. His mouth went instantly dry. Someone must have been hidden behind the screen.

"Turn round, sucker," he heard the voice say.

He rolled over and said, "Clem Mathers."

The man with the protuberant eyes produced a thin smile. "You guess right, boy," he said.

Still keeping his gun on Mitch, the man backed to the wall and fisted it twice. A whoop came from next door.

For a few moments, time seemed to stand still in the room. All three occupants were frozen. Outside, a horse whinnied somewhere and couplings clinked.

"Aaargh!" Mathers shouted and the metal screamed past Mitch's ear and whined as it ricocheted off the metal bedhead.

The gun clattered to the floor.

Mitch uncoiled himself, realizing it could only be seconds before whoever was next door came in. He sprung himself forward, arching his back like a cat, lashing out with his feet. Like lightning he was on top of Mathers, his fingers digging into his windpipe while he smashed him with his right fist.

Mathers desperately tried to roll him, his arms and legs wrapped round him, but Mitch's whole weight and strength was pinning him down. Both men, oblivious to pain, had only one thing on their mind — the gun. Mitch was desperate to get it; the other to prevent him.

Suddenly Mitch felt a wave of fresh air enter the room and then found himself looking down the twin orbs of a shotgun. The fight had stopped.

Both men got up groggily before Mathers vainly swung a roundhouse right in a tired, well-telegraphed arc which Mitch had no problems ducking. The man then lurched on the bed — Maisie screamed — and lay gasping for breath, his chest ruttling. He was, after all, Mitch realized, a man getting on in years.

There was another unreal stillness. Everybody waited for Mathers to revive himself and give the orders.

It was the red-faced man — the snorer — who broke the silence. "Shall I shoot his balls off, Clem?"

Mathers snarled, "Leave that to me." He stood up and bent down wearily to recover his gun which he trained on Mitch's testicles. "No, that comes later. Just pulp his face."

Mitch felt the stunning blow as the shotgun smashed into his cheek and a boot into his shin. Blows rained on him from the two men while Mathers kept him covered. Whilst his hands were above his head trying to fend off the downward blows, he was exposed to the kicks and upward knee.

"Finish it," said Mathers coolly. "We don't want to hurt him, do we?"

The other two men, breathing heavily themselves, added a few more blows for good measure, before dumping him on the bed.

"It wasn't me who betrayed you." It

was the trembling harlot at his side who spoke. "They must have followed you here before."

He gave her a reassuring, thick-lipped, bloody-toothed smile. One of his eyes had almost swollen closed. "I know it," he gasped. "I should have guessed it."

The pain in his jaw, scrotum, kidneys, stomach and head was excruciating. The wound in his side was throbbing intensely and he could feel the blood's wetness. He blamed himself for having less brains than a coot. He should have realized that what had happened was inevitable if he kept returning. But when a man's gone without it for year upon barren year *he sure finds it hard to keep his hands off of it when it's there*. Maguire's words came back to him. He also cursed himself for endangering the girl, bringing her into a fight which was not her own. It crossed his mind that they would not be able to let her live.

"You know what we want!" snapped

Mathers. Blood was trickling from his mouth. "We want what is ours."

"Yeh, we've waited twenty years for it." The livery-stable man had butted in. "We want it bad, Hodder, and we're goin' to git it."

To Mitch, stunned as he was, it was a nightmare of flickering shadows. He was boiling in a cauldron of oil. Three men were dancing round him, their faces greyish and daemonic in the dim, umber light. The eyes of one were those of a ghoulish bullfrog. "Well," said Mathers, "we're waitin'."

"Yeh, we're waitin' and we'll wait for all o' five minutes and then we'll start to smash your teeth in, one by one." It was the fat one, gloating. "And if that don't work, we'll shoot your kneecaps off."

"Then we'll cut your right hand off," said the third man, matter of factly.

"We can surely find something better than that to cut off," sniggered the other, through yellow teeth.

"Well," said Clem, suddenly clapping

his hands together, "ain't we havin' a party? I guess we all oughta kinda get to know each other." He smiled, almost warmly. "We three old friends of your pappy ain't bin properly interduced. This is Mr Martindale." The fat man bowed. "An this 'ere gentleman is Mr Stevens." The man tipped his hat. "And you already know who I am — I'm Clem Mathers — I'm the one you got to worry about, sonny, 'cos these two ain't gonna kill you till I tell 'em."

Then, for the first time, Mathers turned to the girl.

"And this little lovely is Maisie. Yer don't need ter tell me Mitch, I've met her already." The other two guffawed.

He stretched his hand out in the direction of her breast but it never got there, being diverted to fend off her intended facial slap.

"Temper, temper!" he said. "You'd do well to be nice to old Clem," he added, still grinning. "You never know, I might decide to let you live."

"You leave her alone," shouted

Mitch, "she knows nothing."

"Then it's about time I told her," he replied. "You see, my lovely, you might think this 'ere is just another half-breed, just another fella wanting to whip off yer drawers." He flashed his smile again. "But there's two things about him yer might be interested to know. One is he's sweet on you. P'raps yer know it already anyway." His face searched hers. "I could tell it by the things he were sayin' and the things he were doin'." He scratched his chin thoughtfully. "Yeh, I can understand it. It runs in his family, see." Again the others sniggered. "His pa married an Indian. Why? Well I figure some men are jest like that — they need their women to be beneath 'em somehow." The others were highly amused. He winked at them. "I mean beneath 'em in dignity. Let me explain. Yer . . . " he seemed to search for words. "Yer see it kinda make 'em feel big, see. They can't do with no woman bein' as good as them. Else they feel infeery-yor, see!

And I figure this Indian big boy 'ere has kinda got it bad for you.

"I know that 'cos he's started acting plumb stoopid since he met you. He's made it too easy for us. Shall I tell you why he likes you?" She was watching him intently but gave no flicker of an expression. "He likes you, dolly-mop, 'cos every decent woman'll look down on him, turn their noses up at the colour of his skin. Pity really, cos he's a good-lookin' boy. But not you — you're a whore. You're not mighty partickler who you do it with."

The other two were finding this homily richly entertaining. This was their inspired leader talking.

"Now the second thing yer need to know is that this Indian here, he's a very rich man. Yeh, I thought that'd kinda waken you up, sister. Yeh he's got an awful lot o' bucks just awaitin for him — somewhere out in them hills, I reckon." He scrutinized Mitch's battered face, hoping perhaps to have his theory confirmed. "Now that money don't rightly belong to him, see! It rightly belongs to us. We found it, you might say. We found it in a bank a long time ago. And then we lost it, you might say. And now we want it back."

He let all that sink in and then he went on to Mitch. "Now, we're reasonable people. We're not greedy, we're not mean. We're prepared to give you a share."

"What share?"

It was not Mitch who'd spoken but the girl.

"Why one sixth, of course," said Mathers. "That was his pappy's and it's only fair he should get that."

"Take their offer, Mitch," she urged.

"Yeh, one sixth of plenty's plenty," said Martindale.

"It's sure better than nothin'." It was the third man.

"It's surely better than dyin'. Nothin's worth dyin' for," coaxed Mathers.

Mitch was following Maguire's advice: *always let the enemy do the talking.*

A frown indicated that Mathers was losing patience.

"Well I guess that five minutes is up." He spoke resignedly. "I guess you'd better do it, Crag!"

"Sure boss, anythin' in partickler?" Stevens advanced towards Mitch.

"Why cut her nipples off, of course." Her scream was halted by Mitch's upraised hand.

"Wait!" he said. "You leave the girl here and don't ever bother her again and I'll take you for the gold now."

"No deal," said Mathers, back to the grinning again. "She'd talk. Wherever we go she goes till the money's in our hand."

"And then you'll kill us both," said Mitch. Mathers smiled involuntarily again. "That's a chance you'll have to take, mister. It's your best chance."

Mitch had to admit it was his only chance.

"Get a shovel," he said.

The thought struck him, however, that he wouldn't be so much as digging up the gold as digging his own grave.

The three men were hollering and back-slapping.

"We knew you'd see it our way," said Mathers. "We'll ride at first light."

"One thing," said Mitch, "what happened to Clay Beaver?"

There was a burning silence.

"Old Clem's always got an ace in the hole," he said at last.

The three men laughed uproariously.

9

AS the yellow dawn spilled over the eastern hills, four men and one woman bounced down the steep slope in an old buggy.

Mitch was driving, the woman was at his side, thighs apart under her crumpled crimson dress, holding on to him. The buoyant Mathers' gang was in the back.

Maisie caught her breath at the rapidity of going down and glanced at him anxiously, her eyes fringed with dark lashes flickering nervously. Her face, innocent of powder and paint, looked fresher, although there was a pinched look at the corners of her mouth and her eyes were swollen with tiredness.

He hauled the buggy to a halt at the once-familiar tethering, at the bottom under the scanty shade of a gnarled cottonwood tree, next to a tiny trickle of a stream. He jumped down and, pointing to the base of a high outcrop of rock, said one word; "There!"

"You dig," ordered Clem, throwing down the spade.

Although still only first light it was almost hot and Mitch took off his jacket and rolled up his sleeves. For the next quarter of an hour the steady smash of spade on rocky earth twanged on the silence, absorbing the attention of five people in the ordinary and everyday activity of digging a ditch. If Mitch was sweating it was not with the labour but because as soon as his spade hit gold he had outlived his usefulness; he was dead. And no one would bemoan his passing. Certainly not the two men who were standing over him, taut and ripe for action.

The third, Mathers, his head bowed and his tongue continually at work on his dry, white lips, was flexing his hands nervously whilst pacing back and forward.

A sudden flurry of wind sent a long shiver down Mitch's bent back. He straightened up, waist-deep in the hole, and momentarily paused to brush back the damp hair which had fallen over his eyes.

"Get on with it!" snarled Mathers.

Eventually the spade made a plumping thud as it struck something soft. Mathers plunged into the hole and wrested the spade out of Mitch's hand, his large eyes glittering strangely. Then he started to probe with his bony fingers.

He drew out a dirt-encrusted saddlebag and threw it up. It landed dully at the men's feet, obviously empty. Tight-lipped and clammy with fear, Mitch watched five more in quick succession being dragged out and thrown up, with no weight and making no sound. Then Mathers went to it again, probing feverishly, searching for the gold which he hoped had been emptied out.

He straightened up, his face red and horribly contorted. He drew his gun and Mitch saw the sun glinting off the single metallic eye trained on him. Mathers' finger tightened on the trigger.

Nothing happened. Suddenly Mitch's spirits soared, lifted by the realization of what the absence of gold meant. They couldn't kill him — now.

"You can see," he said, seizing his moment, "that no one's dug there for a long time. The earth's packed tight and hard."

"So?" rapped Mathers.

"Well — someone else must of beaten us to it!"

It was an unbelievable thing to say.

"Oh sure, someone just happened to be digging here and found it — then left the saddle-bags."

Mitch looked round uncertainly. "I put the money here myself," he said in a low voice. "My papa stood right there where you lot are standin' now. I remember it as clearly as yesterday."

"And then you came back and moved it later," said Mathers, reasoning verbally, "in case you ever found yourself in this position. So you could play for time like yer doin' now. So it looks like some other critter's moved it. Very smart, Indian! Yer not that dumb."

"Did anybody else know about where you hid it?" It was Maisie, looking thoughtful.

"No one was here except me and pa."

"Could Jed Bellow, fer instance, have seen you?"

"No, no one coulda seen," said Mitch, raising his eyes to the distant rim of the hills. "We made sure o' that. There was nobody within a mile. Jed Bellow was only a kid then, anyway."

"Why did you say Jed Bellow, honey?" asked Mathers, alert as ever.

"Just thinkin," she mused. "He musta come by his money some place."

"He brought it back from out east, din't he?" asked Mitch.

"The only thing he brought back

from out east . . . was me," she said. All eyes turned to her. "He strung me a line about what it'd be like out here. He din't have two cents to his name either out in New York or when he got back." Then her eyes screwed up with menace. "Until he took up with that redhead he married. I always figured he'd got money from her, but where did she get it from, that's what I'd like to know. As soon as she flounced her petticoats at him he became rich and would have nuthin' to do with little ol' Maisie."

She was no longer talking to the group but to herself. Her eyes had glazed over.

"He ruined me. He drove me to all this." She grabbed a handful of her scarlet skirt as if by way of explanation. "He let me walk the streets . . . "

"When he came into all this wealth," said Mathers, "didn't he cut you in for a piece?"

"Nope!"

"Din't you ask him for none?"

117

"Yep!"

"What'd he say?"

"He said he'd got some rich backers and it was all strictly business. He said he'd no ready cash; it was all tied up."

"And he's never given you nothin?"

"I didn't say that," she said, a little cagily. "He's bin generous from time to time when he's in the mood and when he's come to see me. Yeh, he's paid me plenty — especially when he's bin drunk." Her face hardened again. "I wish I coulda thrown it all back in his face. He thinks he can buy me . . . and that's s'posed to make everything right, is it?"

"This ain't leadin' nowhere," put in Stevens. "She's jest spinnin' us a tale."

"Yeh," agreed the fat man, "I ain't interested in Bellow's money. I wanna know where mine is."

"Bellow's got the money — our money," said Mitch. "I've figured it out."

"It's a trick," shouted Stevens.

"Shut up and listen," admonished Mathers. "Awright sonny, you explain some."

"I can't explain it," said Mitch suddenly reticent, "but I swear as sure as day is day and night is night that he's got it. It's got to be him."

"You're not going to take the word o' no Indian, boss?" It was Stevens again.

"It's true," exploded Maisie, "it's got to be him. But how in tarnation did he get it, Mitch?" She looked at Mitch's expressionless face. "Unless — "

"Unless — " said Mathers who'd come to the same conclusion, "unless the redhead knew about it."

"Yeh, right," said Maisie, "and she did, din't she, Mitch?"

"Not exactly," he said, biting his lip; "but, yeh, it wouldn't ha been impossible for her to figure out." He looked round him. "This was our spot. This is where me and Jenny used to come a-courtin'. She might just have

119

been bright enough . . . "

Mathers advanced towards him. "If you're lyin', boy, we're gonna tear you limb from limb!"

"I'm not sayin' nothin'," said Mitch. "I'm not accusin' her. I'm sayin' she mighta figured it out and she might not."

"And she just might have passed her suspicion on to Bellow?"

"It's possible."

"Then," said Mathers with some finality, "I reckon we'd better pay this fella a visit and kinda ask him for what don't rightly belong to him."

"Pah!" The woman shook her head theatrically. "You gotta be outta your mind. He never goes nowhere without bodyguards armed to the teeth. If he's got the gold he's gonna be even more careful now that Mitch's back."

"Anyway," said Mathers, his eyes darting a look from the gaping hole in the ground to search the distance, "that's our problem. I guess we won't be needin' either of you two again. Will we?" He stepped back.

"You might," said Maisie flatly.

"Oh, yeh?"

"You might need me to get round Jed, find out some information from him."

"Mebbe, but set against anything you might come up with, darlin', would be what you might give away to Bellow or someone else. Sorry!"

"You spare the girl and cut me in for a sixth and I'll show you how to get your money." Mitch had spoken hastily.

"Oh, yeh! And how might that be?" Mathers eyed him speculatively.

"Why," Mitch swallowed spasmodically, "we rob Bellow's bank, of course."

"Just like that?" Martindale gave a loud, contemptuous snort.

"Yeh, it's the only way. He'll never give you a dime of it otherwise," said Maisie.

Mathers took off his hat and fanned his perspiring face with it. He was thinking.

"We'd sure need four men for it, boss, it's a big bank," said Stevens. "I mean four includin' Hodder."

They exchanged looks.

"Yeh we'd need four or five for it," he agreed, "but I don't trust Hodder none."

"I'm not gonna double-cross you, am I?" Mitch said. "I bin waitin' twenty years to get my hands on some dough. It's the only thing that's kept me from goin' plum crazy!"

10

"**W**E'LL need a place to hole up," said Mathers. "We've all got to kinda stick together till after the job."

"Yeh; wherever I go, you go," said Martindale to Mitch; "and wherever you go, I go, git it?"

Mitch shrugged. "You can come back to my place," he said with a shadow of a smile.

"Yeh, yer old man's ol' shack will be jest perfect," said Mathers. "Which reminds me of the first rule of this gang. If any one of its members double-crosses the other, the rest swear to hunt him down for the rest of their days. Swear it, boy!"

"Yeh, suits me," said Mitch.

"Swear it!"

"Yeh, OK! I swear to that rule; it makes sense to me."

"What about me?" asked Maisie. "Don't you want me to swear it? Or do you just trust me?"

Mathers smiled. "I don't trust no one, baby. But I'm gonna trust you as far as this; I'm gonna let you . . . "

"You're gonna let me go?" she cut in, brightening.

"No . . . I'm gonna let you stay." His smile broadened to crease the skin at the corner of his eyes. "That's if you're good." He winked; "I mean very good."

"Look, if you let me go I wouldn't tell a soul," she pleaded. "I wouldn't dare."

"Course you would, baby," he said, calmly appraising her; "you'd just put yourself in big with Bellow, wouldn't you? He'd just get a whole army sitting waitin' for us, wouldn't he?"

"I've told you I hate Bellow."

"Yeh, and I heard you," said the leader, "but old Clem — he kinda works on Mathers' law. If you reckon on people acting as they're supposed to, yer dead. People don't. People gen'ly do the opposite of what yer countin' on, partickly when they're in a corner. You'd be sitting there in yer little bedroom and the strain'd get to you as you counted off the hours to the bank robbery." He put his hands up to wave aside the protest she was going to make. "And then you'd start eatin' yer little heart out, thinkin' we was gonna ride off without even givin' you a bean. And yer'd be right, 'cos once we've done it we jest keep movin'. So . . . "

"Oh, shut up," she snapped, "you're really twisted man, you sure are!"

"You stay," said Mathers, uncompromisingly. "When we leave we'll let you go — it'll be a long walk into town and by the time you get there we'll be long gone."

"Oh gee, thanks," she said.

"But 'cos old Clem's not a bad guy and because everybody needs a little summ'n to look forward to, I promise you this . . . " He smiled, benevolence on his countenance. "Pretty soon afterwards I'll personally send you a mint of money, for yer part in all this. That's only fair and old Clem always keeps his word."

His men snickered.

"And you expect me to believe that?" she said incredulously.

"Please yerself, but you'll be kinda agreeably surprised, ma'am, if yer don't." He doffed his hat.

Maisie and Mitch exchanged looks. More powerfully than words, they'd said they'd stick together; they didn't trust Mathers; but he was a hell of a clever guy. You had to hand it to him.

★ ★ ★

With Clem away the two cowboys seemed at a loss to know what to do. They had not accepted Mitch and couldn't talk naturally either to him or to each other in his presence. It was as though they had no course, no direction, nothing by themselves.

The four sat there in a deep, uneasy silence. If anyone shifted slightly three pairs of eyes moved on him, angry that their contemplation of events had been disturbed.

Mitch considered his options carefully. He figured it should be easier to get away from these two without Clem around. But with no gun his chances were still slim — and even if he succeeded, where should he make for?

And would they follow him? Was he now worth following? Probably not unless they believed he'd double-crossed them over the gold.

Then he fell to considering the gold. Rightly it belonged more to him and the Mathers' gang than it did to Jed Bellow. Yet to set that little matter straight they'd have to rob a bank. The chances of getting away were not great. In fact there was a pretty big chance of being gunned down. Gunned down in the street of his home-town! Even that would be better than being caught and sent back . . . The thought of even one more day inside filled his stomach with the blackest of bile.

Maybe it could be done. He began to wonder just how clever Clem was. Could the man really pull it off? He'd done it before, yet that was nearly half a lifetime ago and things had changed. The railway and the telegraph had made bank robbing an even more desperate gamble than it had ever been. But then Mathers did not look the sort to gamble.

11

"IT'S a dead cinch," said Mathers, on his return. His men smiled. "There'll be more money in that bank than we can carry, the amount of business that's goin' on there."

"So when do we do it, boss?" asked Stevens.

"We do it at the very first opportunity . . . maybe the day after tomorrow."

The men's expressions had changed. They looked anxiously at each other.

"Din't we oughta plan this out some?" ventured Stevens, a little hesitantly. "I mean we've been outta this game a long time. Things kinda change. Maybe yer can't just walk into a bank no more and roll 'em over."

"Yeh, right!" agreed the other.

Mathers looked pained. "We're sittin' on a powder keg here." He gave an airy wave. "Four randy guys and one not-too-partickler dame holed up in a small shack like this, not much tucker and you desperate for a drink." He eyed Martindale. "Why, in a matter of hours we'll all want to kill each other."

"But we always used to be so mighty neat and careful," Stevens insisted. "Din't we, Hemp?"

"Well, I reckon Clem knows best, but, yeh, we did used to take more time plannin'."

Mather smiled as usual. "That's 'cos in those days we were well practised and we had the nerve. We could wait. Now we're outta practice and the waitin'll get to us."

"So you're just going to walk in and take it?" said Maisie sarcastically.

"There ain't nothin' to stop us!" retorted Mathers. "There's three old guys work behind the counter but none of 'em is goin' to get brave."

Maisie seemed amused, but Mathers ignored her.

"What about the sheriff?" asked Mitch coolly.

"What about the sheriff?"

"Well, he sure looks a pretty mean dude to me."

"I've already thought of that." Clem's eyes darted to look at Hemp. "We'll get him outta town, don't worry. No detail escapes me."

Suddenly Maisie laughed almost hysterically.

"What in tarnation's the matter with her?" said Mathers.

"There's one thing you obviously don't know, Mr Clever!" She stood up, hands on hips, defiant-looking. "All the big money is kept in a strongroom which is only open for about five minutes, twice a day." She was smirking now at Mathers' look of discomfort. "At about 9.30 Jed arrives with his key. The lock needs two keys, his and the chief cashier's. Jed pops in again in the afternoon if he gets a message more money's needed. He always goes back about four to open up to lock the money away for the night." All eyes had moved away from the girl's face to Mathers'. "So, Mr Clever," she went on, "unless you hit the bank when he's there you've no chance of getting big bucks — and, by the way, when he's there he's always got his two bodyguards outside. Sometimes he's got more, if the bank's loaded."

"How would you know all this?" said Mathers insolently.

She shrugged. "Everybody in town knows. It's common knowledge. You can't miss Jed arrivin' in that silly white buggy of his, in any case."

Mathers continued to look at her mistrustfully. "Why din't you tell us all this before?"

"You never asked me!" she retorted. "Anyway, why should I help you? You don't exactly expect to keep somebody prisoner and them to do you any favour."

"So why you tellin' us now?" put in Martindale.

"'Cos I hate Jed Bellow more than I hate you! 'Cos I kinda got to like this feller, here." She jerked her thumb at

Mitch but didn't look at him. "'Cos I don't want to see him getting all shot up."

Mathers was rolling himself a smoke, quickly and with dextrous fingers. He took a deep lungful, removed a piece of tobacco from his tongue and spoke with exaggerated calmness. "Well, then, the easier way is to go in when Bellow's not there. That way we get whatever loose change is lyin' around. The harder one is to go in when he's there and take as much as we can carry. What do we all think?"

Martindale who seemed to be on the point of bursting — for a drink no doubt — adopted a whingeing tone; "I don't like the idea of being in no bank with two guys outside pinning us down. We could be trapped while a whole loada gunhands arrive."

Stevens agreed and the discussions became intense among the three old-time bank robbers. Finally Mathers turned to Mitch and asked his opinion.

"I say we take Bellow for as much

as we can. Why worry about the hired hands? All we need is for whichever one of us is holdin' the horses to be behind the men. That way they can't protect their backs and pin us in the bank at the same time."

"That's purty good thinkin', boy," said Mathers. "As long as you're not figurin' it's you that's holdin' them there horses." Mitch allowed himself a tight smile. "'Cos," went on Mathers, "that would put you in a position where you could leave us for dead."

"Mathers," said Mitch, "yer forgettin' one thing . . . I hate Bellow even more than Maisie does."

"'Cos he got your girl?" she put in quickly.

"No . . . if he hadn't, somebody else would. I never expected her to wait. We were just kids. No, I guess I hate him 'cos he came by that money even more dishonestly than you fellers did. He stole it without even takin' a risk. And while I rotted in jail . . . " He left the sentence unfinished.

"Yeh, you'll have to kill him, Mitch!" Maisie had spoken. "You'll have to kill him in the bank. That way you've got a chance. If you let him live he'll hound you down until you're dead. He's like that. No one crosses him and gets away with it."

"Yeh," sneered Martindale, "you do that, Hodder. Yer the one that's mighty good at shootin' in cold blood!"

"Anytime you fancy drawin' against me," said Mitch, "you let me know. There'll be nothin' cold blooded about it when I kill you!"

"Yeh, you can count on it, Indian," the man snapped. "Harv Wharton was a buddy of mine and when we've settled matters wi' Bellow, I'm goin' to settle matters wi' you!"

"That's pretty dumb talk," returned Mitch, "even for a whiskey-head like you. Wharton got himself killed and you know it. He didn't stick to your plans. He killed my pa. But for Wharton you'd all have been rich men a long time ago. But for

Wharton I wouldn't have lost twenty years. But . . . "

"Button it!" shouted Mathers loudly, standing up and bringing down his fist on the barrel-head, scattering the cards that his men had been playing earlier. "We get the point. Wharton is dead. Let's all try and stay alive, eh?" He ran a finger down the side of his nose. "The older you get, the harder it becomes. Now Hemp, go and get the bottle that I got you from town out of my saddle-bag and let's get down to details."

★ ★ ★

It was planned for Friday when it seemed likely the bank would have most money in it. Clem was to go into town tomorrow, Thursday; divert the sheriff and his men with an Indian tale, and stay in the hotel.

At five minutes to four Mitch and Stevens would tie up their horses outside the bank and then split up,

Stevens crossing the road as though going to the saloon and Mitch entering the bank. Clem would just appear and follow him in. Clem refused to say where he would appear from and Mitch guessed he'd be staking out the place and if things looked wrong wouldn't show up. Martindale would already be in, opening an account.

As soon as the robbery was going well, that is after the arrival of Bellow, Clem would cross to the window and raise his hat. That was the signal for Stevens to saunter across to the bodyguards, casual-like, and take them by surprise. He'd make them drop their guns but appear to passers-by he was having a friendly conversation with them.

The three would then come out of the bank with the money and they'd hightail out. With the sheriff away they'd get a head start, make for the cross canyons and hole-up in the old shack they'd used for the Bucksville robbery.

It had worked then and it would work now, said Clem. Or would it? To Mitch it seemed unbelievable that a stunt could still work twenty years on. But the gang were in high spirits, bursting with confidence, now that they were committed to it. Mitch began to wonder if they knew something he didn't. Had they got another plan, an entirely different one, one setting him up to take the rap? They seemed too confident. Too confident by far.

He was glad he had a plan of his own.

★ ★ ★

They strolled out together, their hands brushing to start with, and then clasping. They breathed free together under the silvery moon.

They passed over the eerie muskeg flats till the shack was a black knot in the centre of the moon-blanched landscape. Maybe they were trusted or maybe Clem just reckoned they could go nowhere without mounts.

"We could make a run for it," she said, with little conviction.

"No point. There's no place to run."

She turned towards him, her face silvery-white. She looked at the contour of his shadowed face and smiled sadly.

If either was about to speak the other would have known what was going to be said. There was a long silence.

Finally he broke it.

"Do yer . . . er . . . like me some?"

The words had come out. He stood there, half-smiling, his bronze skin almost milk-white in the silver moon. He was vulnerable now, waiting in the lengthening silence. He tried to cover it by adding, "You kinda said back there you did . . . You told Clem that . . . "

"You know it, Mitch . . . " she said, thoughtfully.

There was a reluctance to say more, to open up, unmask. She was used to the physical act first and any talking afterwards. Each quick gesture of her hand smoothing down her dress showed her unease.

He felt he had to say something because she couldn't.

"If . . . " He found his throat had clammed. "If we pull this off . . . Hell, we might do . . . "

"Mitch," she said almost inaudibly, "every night strangers come to you. Or worse, men you know. They're the worst. The ones that come back time and time again. They try to get friendly. They expect . . . they expect more."

Her face looked fresh and soft in the light.

"Don't talk about 'em," he said. "I don't wanna know."

"You've got to know. I've got to tell you why I'm like I am." She seemed to be labouring mightily as though under tremendous strain. Her bosom heaved. He saw that she had started to back away, to shrink from him. She seemed almost to be trembling.

"Sssh!" was all he said as his strong

arms cradled her, drawing her back to him. "Sssh!"

"I do like you Mitch. I . . . guess I love yuh!"

Now it was his turn almost to want to shrink away. The sheer impact of the words had startled him, challenged him. He realized he couldn't say them back.

"Maisie . . . after all this is over . . . "

Now she was shushing him, which she did by placing her forefinger on his lips.

"Don't say," she said. "Don't say. It'll be . . . the death of you."

He laughed. "What will be will be!"

"What I want has never been."

"I know what you want right now and what I want and what's gonna be!" He squeezed her to him.

"Take off yer hat," she whispered, smiling and sinking into the juniper.

He did. She ran her fingers through his hair. She ran them down his body, which still ached from the beating. She touched him and he sprang erect like a sapling released of its weight. In another moment he was on top of her, gazing into her dark, proud eyes which seemed to absorb him.

When his body had gone limp and his head and limbs lay still she said, "Kill him for me."

He did not reply. For the moment he wondered whether she meant Mathers.

"Jed Bellow; I want him dead."

He knew that if he killed him it probably meant the bank-raid had failed.

She grabbed his hair and jerked his head upwards. Her eyes were bright now, and challenging. "Kill him!"

"Yeh, yeh," he said.

"You won't!" She seemed to have lost faith in him. "You're all gonna die."

"If I die I'll take him with me." It was the best he could think of to say.

"I'll do it myself," she said, "if you haven't the balls."

They walked on in silence once more. When they were almost back at the shack they both turned to look at the impenetrable darkness.

"This is it," she said. "This has been our last stand."

"I'll come back for you," he mumbled.

"That's what they all say." She should not have said 'they'. "Men are like . . . islands. They're cut off. They b'long to themselves."

"What are women?"

"Women . . . " she sighed, "women are just crazy."

"So are men," he said.

Her lips had compressed in a grim line. "Kill him for me, Mitch, then I'll know you love me."

12

TWO men, bulky figures with large, folded burlap sacks under their shirts, swaggered into the bank, Mitch in front, Clem behind. Clem peeled off to the right and Mitch went to the other end where Martindale was already in place, his back turned as he bent over the long counter, apparently writing something.

It was red-hot inside the low-ceilinged room. Mitch felt he had to get out quickly. It was an old fear coming back to him. Years ago, when he'd first learnt of his father's profession, he'd had nightmares about such an occasion. Somehow he'd always known that this moment would come. Like father, like son . . .

He had to admire Clem who, having coolly strolled up to join the short queue, had propped himself up against a brass post. He was now raising his hat to a lady who was leaving and flashing her his smile.

It was now several minutes after four and no sign of Bellow. Mitch realized too late the flaw in their plan; there was a limit to the length of time three men could lounge around without causing suspicion. And there were now only three customers ahead of Clem in the queue; a loud and bulky lady, laughing, with the short-sleeved bank teller; a small and wizened man with long, grey, bushy sideburns; and a pretty young woman who also had an equally pretty little girl with her, a kind of miniature version of herself.

Suddenly there was a rattling of hoofs and carriage, growing louder, sharper, and clearer. Then the hollow clomp of high-heeled boots on the boardwalk. The putting down of the heels was so heavy that all the noises of the afternoon — and all of Mitch's destiny — seemed to be absorbed into that self-assured tread.

Mitch's heart was pounding. His wounded side ached. The nape of his neck was prickling. He felt slightly drunk. Somehow everything seemed to be floating in time. Out of the corner of his eye he was aware of the doors drifting open and Bellow entering in slow motion. He was wearing black.

Bellow had gone behind the counter and was standing surveying the great vault of a room. He was looking sharply at Mitch and thinking even though he was speaking in low tones to one of the tellers, a slender, elderly man. The expressions of both men were wary and unfathomable.

Mitch was rigid, his hand hovering near his gun. His mind was over-alert, the muscles in his arm taut as steel rods. He felt the blood tingling and throbbing in his fingers.

Then a feeling came over him again, swamping his senses. It was the weird, pounding feeling he'd had when running down a street all those years ago, forcing him to fling open the bat-wings of a saloon and kill a man. He felt that uncontrollable red, bitter surge now. He would kill Bellow; just co-ordinate his thoughts and his hand, pull the trigger, and watch him keel over. He flexed his fingers and his hand started moving . . .

"Keep calm, everyone!" a voice shouted. Martindale had stepped forwards, his gun drawn. "This is a robbery. We're the Hodder gang and we mean business. We'll shoot anything that moves."

Mitch distantly heard his name being used and realized this was a sort of betrayal. But it mattered not because he wasn't wearing a mask and would be recognized anyway.

"And we don't take prisoners," shouted Clem. "In fact the leader of our gang here . . . " he pointed at Mitch with his gun, "he's well known for gunning people down in cold blood."

Mathers was now behind the counter and jamming his gun into Bellow's midriff. "The keys," he snapped.

Bellow took his out sulkily, glaring at Mitch all the while.

Mitch was amazed at how casual Clem was, how unflustered and apparently unhurried.

Clem barked out another order. "Now get the other key and open the safe!"

Bellow moved slowly and without protest. Advancing towards the oldish man he'd been talking to, he said, "It's all right, Don, you can give me the key."

"Very good, Mr Bellow," murmured the man and produced it from the depths of an inside pocket.

Everything so far had been remarkably calm and matter of fact. It was the sight of the two keys which seemed to galvanize Clem and to animate Martindale.

Mitch realized their casualness had been hiding the fears that if the keys weren't produced somebody might have to be killed and the chances then of

148

getting away or of getting any money would be small.

Now Clem was barking out orders for speed to Bellow who was opening up.

It was probably only a matter of seconds before the large, well-oiled steel door was brought back, but it seemed like a lifetime.

Mitch still had not moved. He was standing there, training his gun on Bellow, fighting back the insistent voice to kill the man who was looking at him in a strangely superior way. It wasn't a look of hate or of fear — or of resentment that his bank was being robbed. It was a look of pleasure — a look which said, "I don't have to fear you now, you sucker; you're going back to the pen for another twenty."

Mitch began to consider that Bellow was probably right. If they all got away, the Mathers' gang could possibly blend into the background, lose themselves in a big city, protected by their new-found money. But a half-caste stood out anywhere; and one famous as leading a gang . . . Mathers had done Bellow's work for him.

At a signal from Clem, Mitch made his first contribution to the proceedings. He advanced to the window and held his hat aloft. Whatever happened out on the street would be vital but the robbers inside the bank could do nothing about it now.

Martindale was at the far end, his great bulk slightly crouched, his legs apart, his gun hand supported by his left hand. He's obviously got the shakes, thought Mitch. Clem was emerging with his bag bulging. He pulled the thongs tight at the neck and held it easily. Though obviously heavy, such riches as it contained seemed to buoy it up in Clem's hands.

"Fill yours pronto," he rapped, "whilst I keep 'em covered!"

"Yes, boss," said Mitch, ironically.

He entered the cavernous room and started flinging wads of greenbacks in his bag. He worked feverishly, greedily, a hundred times the wealth a man might make in a lifetime going through his hands.

He came out and replaced Martindale.

So far everything had proceeded remarkably well. Mitch realized, however, that the tension was increasing all the time. And still Bellow leered at him.

Suddenly the door opened and a small wiry, weasel-faced man entered. For a second he seemed held, frozen, a tiny leaden figure. His face told its own story — he had instantly taken in the whole set-up.

Clem sprang into action, bounding over to the frightened man, his gun fixed on him. Had Clem been slower the man might have shot out of the still-open door, shouting as he did so. But as it was he found himself slung on the floor, staring up at the six-gun.

"Don't open yer mouth," snarled Clem, "unless you want to swallow something nasty!" Jaws clamped tight, the man nodded. Clem took the man's gun and stuck it down his belt.

Martindale emerged with his bag and Clem turned to address his captive audience.

"Right, you keep in here, see. You don't make no noise. You just stay where you are. We're leavin' now."

It was at that precise moment that outside there was, unmistakably, a treble report. The three shots signalled that it was not going to be the perfect crime — something had gone badly wrong. It meant they had to leave now like bats out of hell. And they'd probably be running the gauntlet of men who at this moment were grabbing rifles. No one wanted to see his life savings go galloping out of town.

"You!" yelled Clem to Mitch, "git behind Bellow!" There must be little doubt now who was the real leader of the gang, thought Mitch.

"You're comm' with us, mister," Clem said, digging his gun deep into Bellow's gut. "You just be real good and maybe nobody else'll get shot."

He pushed Bellow out into the street,

sticking close to him, using him as a shield. Mitch and Martindale edged behind them, their guns still trained on the people in the bank.

The street was in a subdued tumult. There was hardly a noise but the silence, after the three loud bangs, was more menacing than the loudness of destruction. Every face was strained and sombre. It was as though for a syllable of time everything had been paralysed, like the momentary stupefied inactivity of a nest of wasps which have suddenly been exposed. Any split second now they would mass and attack.

About twenty yards from the white chariot was Crag Stevens spread-eagled on the ground, his arms and legs flung wide and lifeless. He was dead. Blood had saturated his dun shirt and was pumping out, crimson, into the dust.

In the vehicle was one more lifeless body and another one twitching in the arms of a woman. The woman was Jenny. Armed men were now pouring on to the street from every direction.

All was confusion.

"Get in the wagon," screamed Clem, "and get Bellow and his missis up front. They'll not shoot us then."

"What about the horses?" shouted Martindale. "We'll get nowhere without 'em."

"Yer a sittin' target while yer mount up," was Clem's answer. "Get in the f-ing wagin!"

"I'm not goin' in that!" Martindale's face had twisted horribly.

Surprisingly nimble for a man of his girth he ran towards his horse, his gun drawn, threatening the crowd. As he put his foot in the stirrup four or five shots rang out, presumably from upstairs windows. The horse screamed and fell, its hindlegs writhing. Martindale stood there, his eyes registering disbelief. Then his legs buckled and he sank down to rest like a carcass.

"Jesus!" shouted Bellow, "don't anybody shoot." The writhing eyes no less than the trembling mouth seemed to beseech the onlookers. "No more shooting!" he yelled.

Very slowly the two men edged out behind Bellow to the white carriage.

"Tell 'em to back off," ordered Clem, his left arm round his prisoner's windpipe and his other jamming a gun in his back.

"Aw right, neighbours," shouted Bellow, now as pale as his wife's dress, "we're leavin' now. Don't anyone shoot!"

★ ★ ★

They left town at a stately trot. It was all Mitch could get out of the pair, pulling such a big rig, three men, one woman, two corpses and a quantity of money.

"Get a move on," snapped Clem.

"They won't go no faster," returned Mitch. He was already standing up and lashing the horses; he could do no more.

It was obvious that Martindale had been right. In this contraption they had

155

no chance. His point was now being proved, just as had Clem's — that it was suicide to try to mount up. Either way they were going to die.

And their pursuers knew it. A whole gang of them were just out of gunshot, content just to tag along, waiting to pick their moment.

"Get those bodies out of here," ordered Clem, having grabbed the dead men's guns.

Bellow obliged, the veins standing out in his neck as he heaved the dead weights. His face registered distaste when he found blood on his shirt and hands. Jenny, who was lying back in a sort of swoon, was covered in the red stuff and flies were buzzing round her.

"Well we're gonna get away, or we'll all gonna die," said Clem casually, as though he didn't really care either way. "It's up to you, Mr Bellow. But if I die, you die. I'll take you first." His use of 'mister' had been ironic rather than respectful.

"Those people," said Bellow, drawing a deep breath, "are not gonna let you get away with their money." The fear on his face was genuine. "You're making a big mistake if you think that I can stop them. Most of 'em have no love for me. They'll be quite happy to kill us all and share out the dough between them."

"So yer not a popular guy in yer own town?" said Clem, probing.

"I'm a banker. Nobody likes a banker. They just use my bank 'cos it give their money protection. Now that the bank's been robbed they've no need of me."

"Yeh, they sure look pretty sore at something." Mathers' eyes were everywhere — on the riders, on the people in the wagon, and on the money. Once again he urged Mitch for more speed.

"Take us to my spread," said Bellow, "and my hands will give you protection. We'll come to some arrangement about the money. You won't be able to carry all of it anyway. It'll just slow you down."

Clem laughed bitterly. "Now what kind of dumb head d'y take me for?" He laughed again, a rasping, snarling laugh as though he couldn't believe what he'd heard.

Jenny spoke for the first time. "He's right, mister. It's your only chance. They'll give you horses at the ranch." She seemed to be weighing up the probabilities. "At least you'll have a chance. You've no chance in this buggy."

"Aw right," said Mathers, to Mitch's amazement. "We'll do it! But you two can come along for the ride. Just in case!"

"Now I know you're dumb," said Bellow. "If I go my men'll foller, just like this bunch." He jerked his thumb over yonder. "Just take my wife. We're not goin' to double-cross you if you've got her." She was glaring at him, her nostrils flaring. "I've got to stay behind," he went on, falteringly, "to . . . er . . . keep my men in hand. Without me they'll just add to the strength of the townfolk follerin' yer. That way we'll all end up dead."

Clem laughed again, sardonically. "What d'y think, Indian?"

"He's right," he said. "She's our best insurance. Let Bellow go. He's gonna come after us anyway, but at least he's got the sense to know if he gets too close his wife's gonna get hurt."

"What d'y think, lady?" Clem seemed to be putting it to the vote.

All the while she had been staring strangely at her husband as though trying to fathom his thoughts. Her face had twisted into an unlovely expression.

"Do as you like," she said. "You're gonna do anyway."

"I suppose you two are a happily married couple, like?" said Mathers, his brain as keen as ever. "I suppose yer husband does love yer, lady? He's not about to . . . shall we say . . . sell you out?"

She did not answer immediately. She was still staring at Bellow.

"He loves me enough," she said quietly. "He's not trying to get rid of me, if that's what yer mean."

"'Cos if he is," went on Mathers, "we've been played for suckers and we're as good as dead once we let him go."

"You have my word," said Bellow, "that you'll get a good start."

"Oh gee, that makes us feel a whole lot better," said Clem.

"But I want your word that if you get away, you'll release her unharmed."

He looked at her proudly as though he'd done something noble.

"You're a pretty trusting kind of guy where yer wife's concerned," said Mathers. "I mean it's not every man who'd lend his little lady to a couple of outlaws . . . desperate men. Men who've not seen a woman for . . . well, at least a couple of hours." He laughed so uncontrollably at his own joke that spittle ran down his jaw. "I reckon

160

she's safe with us though, 'cos we're only interested in one thing — getting away with the money; our money!"

Bellow didn't contradict him. "Turn left at the next track, then," he said, his cheeks having returned to their normal pasty colour. "And you can come back to my place."

"Well that's mighty nice of you, stranger," Mathers replied, sarcastic again. "But let me tell you this . . . " his bulging eyes took on real menace, "while we're there my gun's never gonna move from your liver. Get it?" Bellow nodded. "And Hodder's goin to stick close to the dame. Ain't yer Mitch, old pal? And another thing. When we leave you come with us . . . for the first five miles. Then we let you go, but she stays. Get it?" Bellow nodded again. "And if I think yer tryin' in any little way to deal me short I'm gonna kill yer, there and then. 'Cos I've nuthin' to lose mister, except my life. And you'll have done the same. Get it?" Bellow nodded a third time.

"I'm glad we see eye to eye."

He flashed his smile and then lapsed into silence. Once he had made up his mind, he had nothing else to say for the rest of the journey.

13

THEY went through a gate and, as soon as Mitch noticed the name Manywells Ranch, he reined back and slowed to near walking pace.

They were approaching a huge spread, obviously several thousand acres in a good broad valley which had got the best of the local water. Hence its name, and the prime cuts of everything the local country had to offer.

Life was going on peacefully. Well-grazed cattle were roaming freely and a group of cowhands were working on a picket-fence. No one had yet heard about the robbery and killings.

The ranch house was long, sprawling and had the appearance of having been added to on a number of occasions. The pitched roof, contrasting with the white paintwork everywhere, gave it a strangely remote air. It looked cleaner than the ranch houses Mitch had seen and also farther away from the actual business, the barn, the large corrals, the bunk house.

It was the home of a prosperous banker, who kept his hands (and feet) clean, rather than a working farmer. It was the sort of place a man who would ride around in a white chariot would live in. Mitch began to think there must be something more odd about this couple than he had imagined.

Even when they went through the big double gates nothing particularly appeared to be happening. Mr and Mrs Bellow and two men had left. The same number had returned and at approximately the right time.

It was all unreal as the four jumped down and strolled into the ranch.

"OK, Charlie," said Bellow to an old, wizened negro, "you bring all that money inside and take good care of it, d'you hear?"

Behind their backs they heard the

old man suddenly choke out, "Mercy me!"

He'd seen the pools of blood, no doubt.

Clem made himself at home immediately, rasping out orders. "You go in there with her and don't let her out of yer sight. Get it? Don't let her take you in with a flutter of her eyes. Get it?"

Mitch grunted his agreement and then asked what Clem was about to do.

"I've got some talking to do with Bellow. He's got to round his men up to keep off that there posse."

Mitch sat opposite the woman he'd loved when she'd been a girl, when she'd had feelings, before she'd been sucked of blood by the anaemic Bellow.

"Mitch," she said, "I hope you get away. You deserve one break in life." Her voice had risen more than it should have done. "But I don't think you've much of a chance. He'll have you killed."

"Not if you're with us."

"He might not be too bothered about me," she said.

So Mathers' suspicion might have been leading the right way.

"He isn't a husband to you?"

It was a silly question. He regretted it as soon as it had been said. But he couldn't find the words to express his regret.

She appeared to consider it carefully. "He's like any other man. I'm as married as any woman you'll meet," she said sourly. "But Jed is more concerned with power, with money, with paying people back who, he imagines, have double-crossed him than anything else. He's had people killed . . . " she lowered her voice and almost choked on a sob, "for no reason. Men who've maybe looked at me . . . or men whose only crime has been to try to drive a hard bargain with him. He can do anything. He keeps the sheriff in his pocket."

"So why d'y stay with him?"

She stood up to look out of the window.

"I stayed because I've nowhere else to go . . . because I'm married to him . . . because he'd kill me if I left him."

"And yet he's willing to let you go off with us now?"

"That was to save his own skin," she said. "It'll never happen. You don't think you'll walk out of here with all his men standing watching and all those people down on the track?"

"We'll try," he said.

"And if you do, you won't get very far."

"With you we'd have a chance. He couldn't rush us. If he's that jealous he must love you," he reasoned. "And if he loves you he won't want you . . . " He couldn't bring himself to finish the sentence.

"If you take me away, he won't want me back. With his mind he'll imagine every kind of thing happening. He'll be insanely jealous. He'll just want us all killed."

"Then I'll kill him before we leave." He'd spoken coolly and rationally.

"No win either," she said. "If you did that his men would move in. There'd be nothin' to hold them back."

She was holding to her nose a yellow flower which she'd taken out of a vase.

"Jenny," he said using her name for once, "did you visit my pa's grave?"

She turned round and smiled sadly. "Oh, the flowers, you mean? Yes, I put them there every week."

"Why?"

"Dunno. I just thought somebody should."

"Did you feel guilty?"

It was her turn to say, "Why?"

"You showed Bellow the money that my pa had buried, didn't ya?"

"He followed me," she said peevishly. "At first when we were desperate for money I used to go and take a handful now and again. He got wise to it. He followed me. He took it all."

So it was true. Bellow had come by his money just as he suspected, just as Maisie had said.

"Money is bad," was all he said. How many men had died because of that robbery in Bucksville? He'd lost count. And there'd be a few more yet — that was certain.

Suddenly he felt an uncontrollable rage, urging him to go into the next room and bury the contents of his Colt into Bellow's pale flesh. Pay his dues. His fists were clenched.

That would make an end of it.

The door opened and two men entered.

Clem was smiling, that mocking spreading of his lips.

"Well we've come to an arrangement," he said. "We take $25,000 apiece. We ride out tonight from the back of the ranch. We take her with us." He raised his eyebrows at Mitch. "The townsfolk are being told to go back home by Bellow's men. They're being told that Bellow is going to handle it. Their money will be back in the bank tomorrow and the sheriff can come for his prisoners as soon as he gets back from wherever he's been." He raised his eyebrows again. "Not bad, eh, Mitch?"

Not bad, indeed, if it was true. If it was true that is that they'd be riding out at nightfall. If it was true that they were getting their even chance.

For a second Mitch had a surge of confidence in Mathers. Absurdly he was the type to inspire confidence, even though everything, so far, had been a disaster.

Or had it? Maybe Mathers didn't consider losing two of his men the worst thing in the world. Maybe as far as he was concerned everything was going according to some kind of hellish plan to make him rich at whatever cost to others.

But nothing was that simple. Not where greed and jealousy and human life were concerned.

"How d'y know Bellow's men won't be out there tonight waiting to jump us?" he said.

"We're taking his wife, remember."

That was the flaw in Mathers' reasoning — maybe.

"And Bellow for part of the way," said Mitch.

"Right," said Mathers rubbing his hands together. "I say, Mr Bellow, you get your cook to make us something real special. Something to set us up for our journey. Then we'll all sit here real cosy for two hours. I reckon you good people have got a deal of old times to chew over." The mocking laugh again. "Then we set out."

The meal was brought in and it was eaten in virtual silence. Jenny never took her smouldering eyes off her husband throughout. He never once looked at her.

Afterwards she excused herself to go and change. Mitch stood outside her bedroom, following Clem's orders. A few minutes later she came out wearing a buckskin skirt divided in the middle, a jacket of the same material and a man's high-crowned hat. Her hair had been tightly coiled beneath it.

"Will I do?" she said.

"This won't be a picnic," he said.

"Oh no, if it was a picnic we were going to I'd have worn a pretty patterned dress."

Just for a second she had rolled back the years. That was the kind of crack the girl would have made.

14

THE flat valley stretched out all around, an infinite expanse of luminous darkness. There was an eerie silence.

It seemed ridiculous that men fleeing for their lives should encumber themselves with so much. But money and food and arms weighed heavy.

In black relief ahead lay the foothills, hard by the stark mountain range. It was there they were heading, hoping to lose themselves in the cross canyon. Once up there they had hope. There Mitch would back his knowledge against any man's. No white man could know better the endless number of craggy branches, passes and cavernous ways. He and his pa had explored that territory. His pa had disappeared into it time and again and had returned from it. It had been his bolthole.

It was a place you could live and die unknown.

They had left Bellow back down the trail. Clem thought he'd pulled a masterstroke by pitching the banker off his horse, telling him to go back on foot. Mitch was not so sure. He'd sixth-sensed they were being pretty closely followed and it wouldn't be long before Bellow was mounted up again. Would Bellow have the guts for it? Would he, himself, follow, or would he just send on his men? For sure he wouldn't let two outlaws deprive him of $50,000, to say nothing of his wife.

Above everything Mitch hoped and prayed Bellow would come. Without that, without the chance of putting a bullet in him, Mitch would have no appetite for a shoot-out. But what would Bellow's tactic be? How long would he leave it before he rushed them? Because once they were in that canyon they'd have all the advantage, as long as their food and water held out, and Bellow must know that.

Everything depended on how badly Bellow wanted his revenge and whether that crazed his mind to everything else. If his desire for blood was stronger than his wish to keep his wife alive then it was likely that within the next hour he'd rush them.

Mitch was leading the way now, Mathers being content to bring up the rear, behind the girl, trusting that he was being expertly led.

Without these two tagging on Mitch knew he could have gone faster. Night riding was always difficult and dangerous. Most people found it impossible. But to put on speed was only possible for an expert horseman who could feel his way through his animal, alert to its every move.

He stopped and dismounted. The ground beneath, as he suspected, was beginning to get hard and flinty. They were well into the foothills now. He cocked his ear in all directions, listening. But there was no wind to help him. A long way down the trail they must be if they were anywhere. It wasn't, however, the men behind who most worried him. It was those in front. The ones Bellow must have planted if he had any sense. These were the men who would fire in the dark at any sound that moved. He knew they were there. The Indian in him could practically smell them.

"Listen," he breathed, "there's about a mile more of this here climbing then we get to the canyon. If they've got an ambush up ahead that's where they'll hit us."

"It's a chance we've got to take," hissed Mathers.

"There's another way. There's a ridge just over yonder. If we dismount we can haul ourselves up. Getting the horses to follow will be the problem."

"I say we just get on as fast as these nags will take us," said Mathers, "and meet the ambush when we git there. If there is one and I doubt it."

"Listen to him, will yer?" said Jenny.

"Mitch knows what he's talking about. At least half of my husband's men didn't seem to be around tonight when we left." Clem cursed under his breath. "And they sure as hell must be somewhere," she added.

It was the first time he'd heard her swear — that is since he'd come back. She'd sworn like a hell-raiser in her younger days.

"Aw right," croaked Mathers, "I figure this is your show now, boy."

"Give me your handkerchief, Jenny," Mitch said quietly.

She looked surprised, but from her pants pocket produced a small white square of material. He felt its texture and was pleased by its silky feel.

He spread it out on the ground and put his ear to it. It was an old Indian trick and it worked. Some strange property in the material picked up sounds transmitted through the ground and he was grim-faced when he stood up. There was no doubt they were being pretty closely followed.

Mitch walked on, leading his mount. He was searching for something and it did not appear to be where he thought it should be. Twenty years can play tricks in a man's memory.

There should be two huge slabs of rock somewhere. Suddenly his horse snorted and he immediately watched its ears, a sure sign of whether it had picked up a sound. They were pricked. There was no doubt it had.

"Hold the reins," he said to Mathers. He was searching for it. It had to be here somewhere. His hands were probing in the under-bush.

There it was; a kind of gateway between the two giant boulders, hidden beneath twenty years of withered, fallen trees and tumbled rocks.

There was a distant thump now in the darkness, of the hoofs of horses. They were coming slowly but regularly.

"Jesus," yelled Mathers, "what the hell is keeping yer?"

Mitch started to lead his horse in silence. The other two followed, squeezing through the gap, and off the track.

The ground was rising much more steeply. If one of the reluctant horses shied now it would echo through the night, giving the game away that they were off the trail. They had scarcely gone fifty yards in fact before, down below, Jed's men went by. They were travelling in silence and only the horses' hoofs and the occasional clink of horseshoe on stone could be heard. Then in the distance they stopped.

From their position overhead the three could hear the creak of saddle-leather, even the low whispers of voices. Whoever was down there was perhaps wondering if they'd lost their prey. But at length they moved on. They could hardly have suspected anybody on this trail could have got off it.

It was rough climbing, over flint and gravel too loose to grip. Brush cut into them and the horses had to be hauled and goaded.

Mitch was keeping his eye on a

distant peak which jutted out black against the less black sky. They were travelling in zig-zags at one time and lowly skirting the outcrops the next. The hill was too steep to tackle head-on.

It was, Mitch reckoned, exactly the sort of condition in which a horse would spring a shoe or, even worse, go lame. But there was no other way now. No way down until they were right at the top.

They continued their climb, Clem breathing heavily and cursing. At last he hissed for them to stop. He took down his canteen and drank greedily, gulping the water. Jenny took the opportunity to do the same.

That was not the way to do things, Mitch knew, but there was no point in telling thirsty people to save their water.

He took a small mouthful from his own canteen and rinsed it round his mouth, gargling it slowly down his gullet to get every drop of lubrication out of it on to his parched throat.

The night was cool now with the breeze that blows just before dawn. First light was only half an hour away. Unless they were over the peak by then, the three black riders would be silhouetted for all the world to see.

It was a race against time. Unless they got beyond that peak in these last murky minutes their single, slim advantage was lost.

Mitch reckoned that by now their pursuers would be pretty near to meeting up with the men who lay in ambush. As soon as that happened they'd figure out that somehow the fugitives had turned off. They'd backtrack and by the light of dawn pick up their trail. They wouldn't even be slowed down by following. They'd just go back up the main trail, knowing that eventually three people would have to come out in the canyon.

He didn't have to explain it to the others. Mathers knew. He was urging them on now for dear life.

They were going uphill now, the sweat blinding them, their lungs bursting. They had to make it.

The little stifled whoop Mathers gave when eventually they crossed over the skyline and started nudging downwards said everything.

With the morning's first pale light throwing an ashen pallor on to their faces the three swapped glances. Sweat beaded their foreheads and glistened on their upper lips. As they descended into a quiet brightening radiance Mathers slapped Mitch on the back, as though signalling a bond between them.

"By God," he said, "I'm glad it was the other two that got killed and not you. There's no way I'd have got up that mountain without you. It was a miracle we made it."

"Yeh," said Mitch, "I don't think any of us would have been bone-headed enough to try it in the light."

Even Jenny, drawn and wan-faced, laughed at the humour of what Mitch had said. But it was a laugh instantly stifled at the realization of the bitter undertone.

Along the canyon they cantered. Sometimes they were in the open, but generally they seemed to be following the trails of wild animals and were swamped and choked with the thick powdery growth of bushes and gnarled trees, cottonwood, box elder and the hard, slim ash which ripped through the skin. Every mile made them that much safer but seemed to increase their jitteriness. The nearer they got to safety the greater the nerves increased as they realized it could be done but equally some mishap — a horse's torn tendon, for instance — would be enough to kill them.

But Bellow's horses proved dependable and, as hour after hour slipped by, hunger and saddle-soreness more than fear of capture began to nag at them.

The air was chilly and they were wet with sweat after the mountain climbing. Jenny shivered.

"By God we've done it," said Clem

as they reined in and flung themselves on the dust next to a standing pool of silver water.

They didn't even bother to hobble their horses. Animals as tired as these would not wander away — even after they'd drunk their fill.

Ten minutes later they were mounted again, and virtually asleep in the saddle as the horses pressed on, now at a snail-pace.

Five more minutes and the first turn-off would take them into the labyrinthine world of branch canyons which Mitch had once known. Would he still know it? Because if he didn't they'd end up as three corpses for the buzzards to feed on. Now that they were almost there this was the fear that nagged him. The chaos of paths, gorges and animal trails that had been so clear to him once, suddenly seemed to fade from memory as he was about to confront them.

No one spoke as they pulled off. They kept on in gloomy silence. Their pace was almost non-existent as they threaded their way, hangdog figures startled by dropping rocks and goaded by needle-armoured cacti.

The turgid branches had great steep sabre-toothed sides, sometimes the passage was so narrow the riders had to slit their way through in single file and then it would spread wide and flat to the hardest of country, enmeshed with brush and unforgiving scrub. There were standing salt pools of grey, sheer water, fringed with the same cottonwood, box elder, sprawling ash tangles. Stinging flies, the size of wasps, buzzed angrily, carving through the air and crawling over the mouth and eyes no matter how much the riders flapped at them. It seemed as if none who entered this hell could ever come out of it.

There were amazing shifts of landscape, rising from the chaos of rock at its narrowest, and spreading wide to a desert of rutted popcorn sands, spiked with thorns. The heat-waves were suffocatingly intense where the going was broad; the narrow gullies were cooler but the riding was crueller, obstructions having to be ridden through, not gone round, shredding human and animal flesh alike . . .

The pattering of hoofs beneath them went on for mile after treacherous mile. They rode on mostly now in single file, their mouths and noses covered for a little protection against the hot dust and flies. No one spoke, but they were bonded faster by their ordeal than words could express.

They halted frequently while Mitch, his face fierce with concentration, checked their bearings. When they stopped the silence was hot and heavy and unnatural. Their gazes passed unseeingly over each other.

Their canteens were getting empty now, the sloshing of water loudening as it lessened in content. Mitch felt drained of all knowledge. It was only will power that kept him going. His brain was dull and each decision tortured him. Every landmark seemed to blur in front of his very eyes.

15

THREE ragged figures arrived, looking as if they'd run the gauntlet of a plague of locusts. They were bloodied and filthy. The girl's shredded buckskins were white, no longer brown. She took off her wide-brimmed hat for the first time and let down her rich hair. The straggling curls were flaked with travel dust; nevertheless there was a golden aura about her as she stood there in the orange light. By contrast the men, their chins grey and stubbly, their hair dishevelled, looked saturnine. Jenny smiled reluctantly at them.

The long, narrow shack was unchanged. Mitch had visited it with his pa, and to Clem, who had holed-up in it on many occasions, it was like a home from home.

It was a place they could stay

forever — or at least till their tucker ran out. Water was now no problem. There was a thin mountain spring running alongside the shack. Without that it would never have been built.

They all laughed, not that anything was funny, and though it hurt their parched throats. It was just an expression of relief. Here was, if nothing more, the sleep their aching minds and bodies had craved. Here was an end to the rough, hard trail.

If anybody found them here, well, that was it. They'd die here. They were going no further. They had promised themselves this retreat and here they were — at the last gasp.

Their swollen, shapeless faces, their grey, sunken eyes, proclaimed one thing. Sleep was more important to them now than gold, than food, than anything. Except water.

They staggered from their horses and lay on the ground, their skulls pounding as they gulped from the stream.

Mitch lay there, panting. You can't drink and breathe at the same time and he'd been more interested in water than air.

He lay there in the stream, muddy and drenched, exhausted and happy. The air seemed alive with the lapping horses, the trickling of spring water and the buzzing of flies.

Then something seemed to be happening in his brain. Was he so tired that his mind was playing tricks on him or was that, in the soft mud, the fresh imprint of a hoof?

Almost immediately the water diverted by their own drinking horses had covered it up. Perhaps it was one of their prints. It had to be! There was no way Bellow's mob could have even followed them here, never mind got here before them.

He looked up and was amazed to see tears streaming down Jenny's face. They seemed to lend an unearthly brightness to the swollen smile she was giving him.

"Jenny," he said.

"Yeh?" "Nothing. Just Jenny, that's all."

"I never thought you had a chance," she was saying. "I never thought we'd make it." Then her smile faded. Her face clouded. "Y'don't think they can foller us here?"

"No," he said flatly. "They've no chance." It seemed all about chances now, and theirs looked promising.

"No," put in Mathers, "no one knows about this place. It's never let me down. I once holed up in it for six months."

"Six months," she said, her eyes widening. "Six months."

"Yes, lady," he said. "But your husband's not gonna look that long. He ain't that strong. Now me . . . " He was gloating now. "I waited twenty years to git what I wanted!"

They hauled themselves to their feet and tottered up the wooden steps. Mitch leaned his weight against the door and they filed in and flung themselves on a bench under the window.

Then they saw him. He was towering back in the shadows, all 200 pounds of him.

It was Sheriff Tex Brownlee and he was grinning horribly. His pistol was drawn and cocked.

"What kept you?" he said.

It was Jenny who spoke.

"Tex," she said, "listen to me. These men are not bad . . . they all took what more belonged to them than to Jed. Take me back and let them go. We'll see you get a share of the money."

Then Mathers started to laugh, loudly, horribly, almost hysterically. "Clay, you old son-of-a-gun," he said, punching the air in delight, "you might have got the coffee-pot on the boil for us."

He was standing up when the sheriff's gun roared, filling the air with the pungent smell. A splinter had formed in the bench.

"Stay where you are, Clem!" he

snarled. "I'm running this now."

"Clay!" said Clem, "don't do this to me. You can have yer fair share — like we agreed."

"Shut up!" rapped the sheriff, "let me do the talkin'!" He spat tobacco juice and then wiped his mouth with the back of his left hand. "I don't want no fair share. I want it all! I've earned it. I've been working in that town for twenty years. What have you been doin' all that time? Not much eh? It was your idea that I ran for sheriff wasn't it? Your great idea eh! Have a man in Ashton you said, 'cos one day that's where it's all gonna end. Well I'll tell you something, Clem . . ."

Mathers held up his hand. "Shut up, Clay, the more you say now to these two the worse it's gonna be."

"Bull!" said the sheriff. "These two don't mean nothing. They're dead and so are you. I wanna go back to Ashton; I'm kinda respected there." He tapped his badge. "I've got a position. A man could be fine and dandy in his old age in a place like that with a whole heap a money stashed away."

"You can still do that," wheedled Mathers. Mitch noticed Clem had unbuttoned his jacket and was slyly endeavouring to get it behind his holster. "You can go back with your share and no one will be the wiser."

"This 'ere fine lady would blab to her husband."

Mathers smiled in his old way. "But yer gonna kill her, Clay . . . and the Indian. But old Clem, yer old buddy, yer not gonna kill him . . . "

It was at that second that Mathers went for his gun — and Mitch went for his. Three shots rang out just about simultaneously.

There had been three good gunmen. Now there was but one. The big man slumped, spliced through the heart by Mitch's shot. He'd aimed for that. The big man had a stomach wound where Mathers had got him.

Clem was dying. The sheriff's shot had pierced him through the throat.

Blood and froth came gurgling out. He lay back on the bench, twitching, his eyes almost bursting out of their sockets. He was trying to speak but could say nothing. Then his eyes dimmed and very slowly closed.

They left the room unable to stand the reek of the burned powder, the blood and the death.

They stood there in the clean air, looking at the magnificent aerial world of jutting crags and sheer, steely-streaked peaks, which took on amazing variations of colour when bathed in sunlight.

"D'y know," she said, putting her arms round his waist and looking up into his face.

"What?" he said softly, nuzzling her neck and beginning to undo her at the cleavage.

"Well, I've always had a fancy to go to St Louis."

"St Louis?" he said. "What's wrong with New Orleans?"

"St Louis or New Orleans," she said.

"Ain't it hard?" she drawled.

"What?"

"Workin' for old man Martin. He never gives you a minute."

Then he bit her neck and they'd done talking.

Epilogue

THE air was shattered by the shrill steam-whistle. A flock of grey-brown ducks took off, beating the sluggish river with their wings.

The paddle-steamer's engine was clanking. A bell clanged repeatedly and the paddles whirred in reverse, as the *Louisiana Lady* bumped alongside the crowded wooden landing jetty.

"Welcome to Noo Orlons," shouted a negro, his pearly teeth flashing in the bright sun.

The passengers massed on the landing side shrieked and whooped in delight, their long journey over.

Mitch thought his was just beginning. He looked at Jenny. Her eyes were excitedly taking in the waterfront, the conglomeration of wooden buildings on stilts rising out of the Mississippi mud.

He turned to look back up the

river. Intently, he watched the ducks swerve, seem to hover, then flop down gracelessly on a mudbank.

They let all the passengers disembark. There was no hurry. It was four o'clock and they had the whole evening to find lodgings.

His thoughts went back to Ashton. He could see it all as clearly as if he was standing there in the main street. Bellow would be coming out of the bank any time now and getting into his white buggy. He would probably have doubled his bodyguard.

Maybe he would glance across and meet for a second a face at a window before the curtain was instantly lowered. Maybe that night there would be a half-smoked black cheroot in Maisie's ashtray.

Maisie! He had not forgotten her. Tomorrow, when the telegraph opened he would wire her some money.

She ought to enjoy life; what remained of it. One day they'd drag her off. She'd have killed Bellow.

FIGHTING RAMROD
Charles N. Heckelmann

Most men would have cut their losses, but Frazer counted the bullets in his guns and said he'd soak the range in blood before he'd give up another inch of what was his.

LONE GUN
Eric Allen

Smoke Blackbird had been away too long. The Lequires had seized the Blackbird farm, forcing the Indians and settlers off, and no one seemed willing to fight! He had to fight alone.

THE THIRD RIDER
Barry Cord

Mel Rawlins wasn't going to let anything stand in his way. His father was murdered, his two brothers gone. Now Mel rode for vengeance.

ARIZONA DRIFTERS
W. C. Tuttle

When drifting Dutton and Lonnie Steelman decide to become partners they find that they have a common enemy in the formidable Thurston brothers.

TOMBSTONE
Matt Braun

Wells Fargo paid Luke Starbuck to outgun the silver-thieving stagecoach gang at Tombstone. Before long Luke can see the only thing bearing fruit in this eldorado will be the gallows tree.

HIGH BORDER RIDERS
Lee Floren

Buckshot McKee and Tortilla Joe cut the trail of a border tough who was running Mexican beef into Texas. They stopped the smuggler in his tracks.

BRETT RANDALL, GAMBLER
E. B. Mann

Larry Day had the choice of running away from the law or of assuming a dead man's place. No matter what he decided he was bound to end up dead.

THE GUNSHARP
William R. Cox

The Eggerleys weren't very smart. They trained their sights on Will Carney and Arizona's biggest blood bath began.

THE DEPUTY OF SAN RIANO
Lawrence A. Keating and
Al. P. Nelson

When a man fell dead from his horse, Ed Grant was spotted riding away from the scene. The deputy sheriff rode out after him and came up against everything from gunfire to dynamite.